Mission to Mankind

Christian fundamentals have no planetary boundaries

The Worth and Dignity of Humanity

Terry Dodd

Mission to Mankind
Published by Yawn's Publishing
2555 Marietta Hwy, Suite 103
Canton, GA 30114
www.yawnsbooks.com

Library of Congress Control Number: 2022919349

ISBN: 978-1-954617-58-2

Printed in the United States

FOREWORD

Mission to Mankind is an intriguing and fascinating account of intergalactic travel, futuristic technology, family dynamics and most importantly, communicating the Gospel message. Terry has an entertaining and engaging writing style that always leaves you wanting more.

The dominant theme of the book can be summed–up with these words: salvation, discipleship and missions. Terry carefully and accurately develops these Christian realities through his characters and their conversations and interactions about universal sin, the need for a Savior and the fact that Jesus is the only Way. Special attention is also given to the oft-neglected aspect of what needs to happen after salvation.

An equally important part of the Christian experience is sharing one's faith with others, often in distant places – missions! This, likewise, is a prominent element of Terry's story. This book communicates many of the basics of the Christian faith, but does so in a relevant, interesting and certainly creative fashion.

You will enjoy this read and be blessed by it.

Dr. Larry Aultman
Missions and Adult Education Pastor
First Redeemer Church

CONTENTS

DEDICATION and PREFACE

I dedicate this work to my wife of more than sixteen years. Helga has been my love since the first day we met at one of our church's Stephen Ministry sessions, when God clearly told me she would be my new helper. Within a year of having lost to cancer the 45-year first love of my life and the mother of my three children, Helga not only became my wife and rescuer, but she also brought to the table her German-speaking fluency and 20-plus years of administrative assistance to three different CEO's of a major international corporation.

I continue this dedication to Helga and her professional administrative experience by paraphrasing something from a book publisher: "Copyediting is the glorious opportunity to be present at the *creation* of something. It is a matter of facilitating clarity and understanding while at the same time allowing the author to get away with a lot, as long as it is clear."

And lastly in this note of dedication to my wife, I can hardly omit reflecting on a special quality, of which I am the chief beneficiary, in spite of my finicky tastes: That would be her motivation to search for and execute the next interesting cooking or baking recipe!

I consider myself first of all to be a Christian; secondly, a husband and father; and thirdly, a writer. I trust that all three of these attributes come into play in my daily life, aims and relationships.

I believe the three most important three-word phrase in the English language is "In beginning God." The eternal God created everything on Earth, as well as the universe's billions of galaxies. With respect to "race," the often unstated axiom is that there is only one species of intelligence made in the Creator's image: mankind (*Homo sapiens*).

1

As for evolution, it is only possible within its kinds, i.e. microevolution: *Let the earth bring forth the living creature after its kind, cattle, and creeping thing, and beast of the earth after its kind* (Genesis 1:24).

With respect to salvation, the Mosaic Law never anticipated a resurrection from the grave. When humanity sinned under the Mosaic Law, humanity died. When Jesus died on the cross of Calvary, it was because of the Law's demand that "the soul that sinneth (separated from God), it shall die" (Ezekiel 18:4). What does that verse mean? Everyone is born into this world spiritually dead. Those who decide for Christ and accept the salvation He offers become spiritually alive (born again). Those who never accept Christ as LORD and Savior are physically alive, but continue in spiritual death!

As the illustrious M.J. Rosenthal (1935-2022) put it, "to provide a way out from this death sentence, Jesus takes our place as our substitute and offers His life in place of ours, providing for us the worth and dignity we do not deserve."

The glorious, artful illustration on the front cover of this book—which I captured from the internet, and so note in my "sources cited" credits—included an interesting viewer's online comment: "A picture like this makes me question my agnostic atheism." A bit more profoundly expressed, however, are the words written some 2,000 years before Christ, in the book of Job: "God . . . hangs the earth upon nothing."

Rosenthal also reminds us of what the writer of Hebrews said on this subject: "Through faith we understand that the worlds were framed by the word of God, so that the things which are seen were not made of things which do appear." Thus was God's way of addressing for humans the molecular, atomic nature of the universe.

Lastly, I want to thank two people in particular: First of all, Dr. Larry Aultman, for graciously providing me with a foreword. Dr. Aultman is not only the indefatigable missions pastor for First Redeemer Church, having preached to thousands of people all over the world and seeing to the nearly fifty Redeemer churches planted worldwide, but he also personally conducted believer's baptism for my wife and I.

I also want to thank Jay McSwain for providing me with a back cover endorsement of this book. Jay is the author of *Finding Your Place in Life and Ministry*, a champion of promoting Christian discipleship, and Chaplain to the Atlanta Braves.

Before we begin this story in earnest, however, allow me to use the prologue for this novel to broadly review my three-book Christian sci-fi series which I refer to as the Gam'man Trilogy. These titles preceded this fourth and final book of the series, which you have blessed me with your intention of reading.

PROLOGUE

Relevant Notes from Book One: *Mirror Magic*

The trilogy begins with geologist-become-advertising prodigy Ben Walker, whose curiosity about competitor Mirror Magic's illogical corner on the promotional products market is consuming him. At the same time, two unlikely characters, the aforementioned Gam'man and P. Chesser enter the picture. They are two rascally former residents of Jun'or and decades-earlier escapees from their lifetime sentences to white-collar incarceration on one of planet Jun'or's two moons.

They, too, become seriously concerned about Mirror Magic, but only because of one Phil Sloann, their estranged former colleague-in-crime and fellow escapee fifty years earlier. He is currently the evil genius CEO of Mirror Magic. Jun'or, along with Andivoli, is one of the two long-ago earth-colonized planets.

The murderous secret to MM's out-of-this world subliminal advertising process utilizing commercial mirrors is discovered by Walker and his female cohort, Amanda. They successfully enlist Gam'man and Chesser with a plan to sabotage the maverick Sloann's production template for the incredible subliminal messaging process which, although printed invisibly, can nevertheless register information with the mind. Chesser is killed in the effort, but not before he creates in his wake electronic messaging havoc for Mirror Magic.

The scheme to control America's upcoming presidential election is dashed, but MM survives for another three years. During that time, Chesser's masked subliminal electronic "fix" buries the new ownership by replacing all advertisers' messages with a benevolent campaign on be-half of mankind.

Relevant Notes from Book Two: *Ultimate Encounter*

The trilogy continues with media frenzy over an in-creasing public outcry about the dramatic increase in UFO sightings, including an upsurge in emotional claims of reported personal atrocities committed by seeming ex-traterrestrials. The United States Air Force seeks out Gam'man—the only known reputed "extraterrestrial" liv-ing on Earth—in hopes they can recruit him to establish the first reciprocal communication with the objectionable Earth-orbit ETs whose apparent, un-earthly technological presence has long been recorded. Even before he is fully underway with the assignment, Gam'man finds himself publicly—if uncomfortably—acclaimed hero-to-the-world.

It is widely believed that Gam'man, having demon-strated a telepathic ability, should thus reasonably be able to accomplish reciprocal communication with the in-terlopers. He carefully crafts a telepathic broadcast to the ETs which he correctly presumes to also be telepathic. His thinking is that the right kind of message might find a curious maverick among the ET's lot.

After days of tedious and exhausting attempts, he fi-nally receives a single response from a teenaged female who reluctantly gives her name as Son-tu. She does in-deed have a question for him. Does the telepathic sender know the Creator? Gam'man, not being a man of God at the time, is blind-sided. Out of a combination of trepida-tion and responsibility for the young female's unique cir-cumstances, he undertakes an intense study of the faith. Within a short time he falls to his knees in asking the Almighty Creator that if He is truly there, would He show Himself.

God reveals Himself in a way which allows Gam'man to gain renewed purpose in life. He responds to Son-tu and offers to become her mentor. They meet at a remote location at the edge of the North side of the Grand Canyon.

Shortly thereafter, and on a literal world stage, Son-tu identifies herself and her fellow visitors as being from the Earth-colonized planet Andivoli. Still holding court, she staggers her world-wide audience with a factual statement that she is the product of a clinical reproduction between a once-abducted Earther (Gam'man's bastard son) and an Andivolean donor egg. Translated, she is Gam'man's biologic granddaughter.

Over succeeding weeks, Gam'man gains the opportunity for a face-to-face meeting with a small contingent of Son-tu's Andivolean elders. Amazingly, they agree to finally 'coming out.' This event happens during what Gam'man vaguely advises the Elders will be a public convocation. In reality, the *convocation* is the 7th inning of the opening game of a baseball World Series in Atlanta. Gam'man has the hope of somehow satisfying human eyes, ears, and hearts that the intruders are an essentially benign (if undesired) presence in and around Earth's orbit.

Relevant Notes from Book Three:
Unto the Heavens

The concluding story of the trilogy is a metaphor for earth's evils and its rejection of the Gospel. It is further revealed that the Andivolean Elders are literally beholden to Satan, but with all that Son-tu would accomplish, she would seem to be kicking him in the shins.

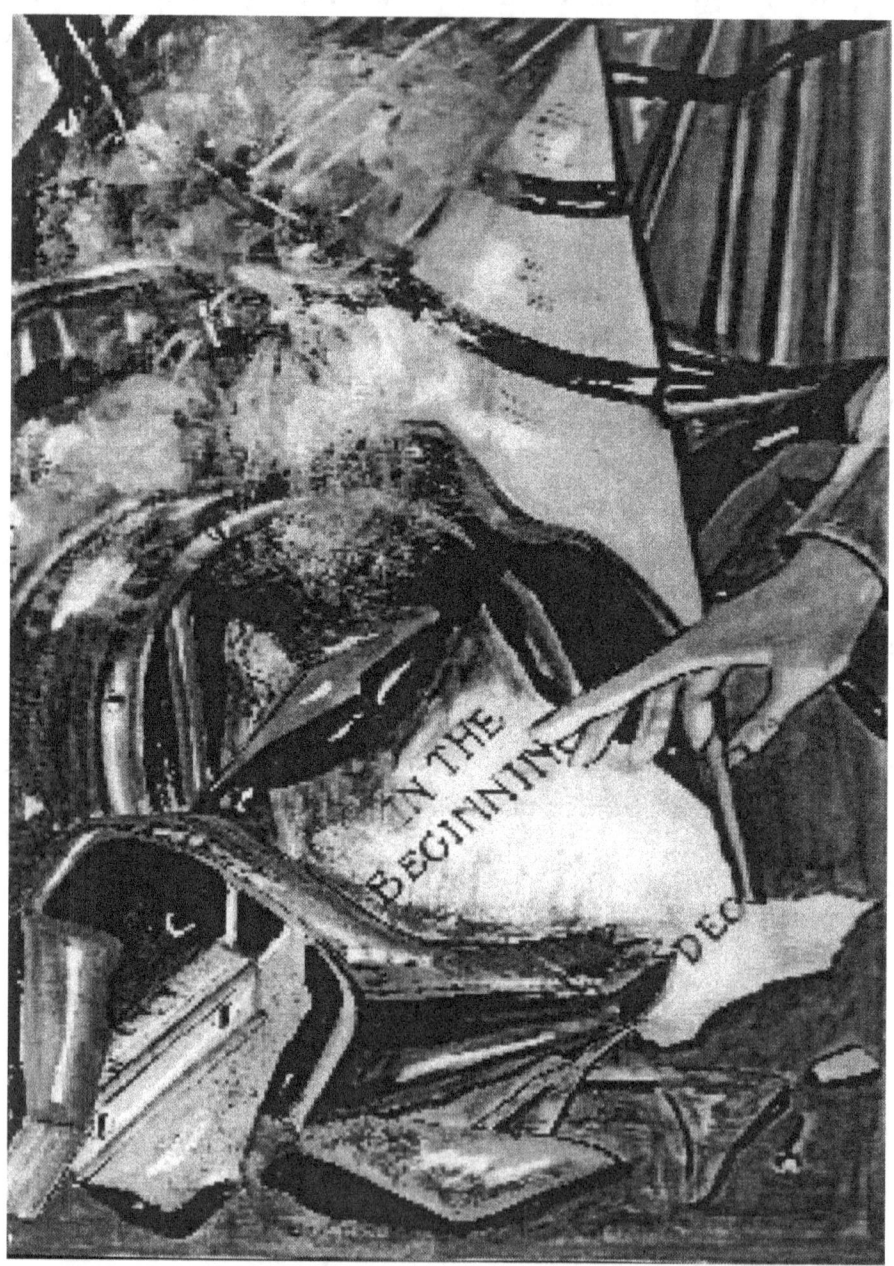

The origin of man's presumption of Jun'or's mysterious prophet, DEO

She astonishes Gam'man with two statements: One, she feels called of God to evangelize the people on her grandfather's pagan colonized planet, Jun'or; two, she wants him to accompany her. He demurs, wary of what he stated would require a seven-year return trip in his long-hidden, half-century old space craft. The reluctant wayfarer is also concerned with the minor matter of being a fugitive from Jun'or's moon-side incarceration. Son-tu persists, explaining that she plans to commandeer a small, two-passenger, Andivolean gravity-driven craft capable of making the trip in a ten-day hyper-space jump.

Gam'man says he will reconsider the entreaty by seeking God's will. A major part of such reconsideration has to do with having lost his beloved late-in-life wife. After a short period he shares his decision with Son-tu: "It has come to this: Is there one last big adventure in which I should engage before I fall off the perch?'

There was! He agrees to accompany Son-tu in traversing to a dark corner of the galaxy to support her goal of "planting the message of the gospel where her most immediate forbearers bloomed."

En route to Jun'or, two sinister Andivolean Elders make a dramatic, if awkward teleportation appearance aboard the cramped ship. Gam'man is flabbergasted, but Son-tu attributes the capability to their in-common full-blooded Andivolean genetics. They threaten dire consequences if Son-tu does not immediately return with them to the Andivolean fold. She boldly calls them out and sends the pair packing.

On Jun'or, Gam'man is surprisingly successful in making telepathic contact with Wy Chesser, grandson of his deceased former colleague, P. Chesser. Surprisingly, he is the leader of a small Christian group called the Rimerian Movement. They not only place their faith in a

Creator, but also claim they are in possession of a dec-
ades-old document from a single page of the Holy Bible.

The unlikely genesis of such a claim is learned: The
sacred document is the result of retrieval from a much
earlier UAP (Unidentified Aerial Phenomena) crash on
Earth's moon. It is believed to have been written by a
prophet named DEO. In reality, the name is merely three
letters from a fire-singed page of a Bible left on the moon
by an Earth astronaut who was also a member of the
Gideon's Society, thus the name DEO. All of this took
place sometime after Earth's secular colonization of
Jun'or.

Son-tu's initial gospel message to the people of Jun'or
is well-received by a small segment of a still hugely secular population. Apparently, two of the members of the colonizing population had aberrant genetics which resulted
in a form of mental telepathy, carrying forward in succeeding full-blooded generations.

Because such a trait impacts individual thought pri-
vacy, it quickly became seen as a curse. Out of the people's fervent hope of relief they now want to anoint Son-tu
as Savior. Things quickly turn sour for the newcomers,
however, when the cultural opposition charges heresy for
attacking the greater population's preference for pursuit
of self-gratification.

Son-tu finds serious interest in a personal male security admirer, one Agent Boxxton. After a short, initial period of positive interaction with Son-tu and Gam'man, he
dramatically but inexplicably expires. Suspecting foul
play, Son-tu persists in gaining admission to the hospital
morgue. She then spreads herself out over Boxx as he lay
on a morgue slab, telling him—in the name of the Almighty Creator—to open his eyes and arise. As with the
instance of Paul's reanimation of the young Eutychus in
Acts 20: 6-12, Boxx is miraculously reanimated.

Son-tu continues to lead the movement, and in a vision she understands that because of Jun'or's gross rebellion against God the laws of electronics on the planet will be suspended. She publicly announces that prediction which then comes to pass. Chaos ensues.

The evil Andivolean elders teleport themselves to Jun'or, but this time they bring along a new ally. He is none other than Sloann Jr. He is the similarly-minded, vengeful son of Gam'man's former nemesis on Earth. To further complicate matters for the home team, the bad guys capture Junor's two evangelical Rimerian Movement's leaders, demanding the life of either Gam'man or Son-tu in exchange; else they will eliminate both of the captives.

Son-tu volunteers, but Gam'man overrides her decision in substituting himself. Sadly, while in captivity, he passes. Life on Jun'or begins to devolve and the cycle of Christian faith waxes and wanes, just as it has on Earth both before and after Christ's first coming. This, then, ends the Gam'man trilogy with Son-tu feeling lost with respect to Gam'man's passing and her new calling apparently ended.

ADDITIONAL REFLECTIONS

Like any writer, I have often been asked casual questions about my writing.

One particularly interesting question is this: "What is your greatest reward from the writing process?" Without deliberation I can say it is all about the actual writing rather than finding a publisher, marketing, or even book sales. My process of producing a manuscript to deliver to my publisher—the last ten of my sixteen titles being with the same house—is enjoyably working through ten or so drafts of writing, re-writing, editing, and proofing. In the case of fiction, it is the further excitement of knowing my characters well enough to understand their thoughts and motivation. And while mainstream publishing would surely yield greater sales, self-publishing is not only light-years faster, but immensely less stressful. My advice concerning someone's interest in earning a living by writing is that one would be better off studying to become a plumber.

In the case of *this* story, my intention has simply been to write a science-fiction/Christian apologetic. When I was fortunate enough to pick-up a well-respected East coast sci-fi literary agent for the Gam'man trilogy in 2015, I wrote revisions for all three of those books under new titles. Two years later the agent soft-pedaled my release from our contract, saying that although her publishers—both Christian and science-fiction—liked my writing style, they wanted their ideals met. In other words, they didn't like my combining science-fiction with Christian faith.

Neither was I willing to compromise. To those who ask whether my latest book is Christian or science-fiction, my answer is that it is a mutable compound of both. Writing success for me has always been following my style and motivation, rather than publisher—or even general reader—preference.

The Bible does not address planetary boundaries relative to Christian fundamentals. My story simply deals with the worth and dignity of humanity, wherever found. I thus thank god and take modest pride in production of sixteen self-published Christian books.

I further state a fundamental and foundational tenet concerning my personal *young earth creationism* (YEC) belief: The Earth and its lifeforms were created in their present make-up by supernatural acts of the God of Abraham between approximately 6,000 and 10,000 years ago.

YEC is thus based on the Christian faith and the inerrancy of certain literal interpretations of the Book of Genesis

From this point, I paraphrase a beautifully worded statement: "After the biblical worldwide flood had receded and the land had dried out, Noah stepped out of the ark onto an earth devoid of human life. But God gave him a reassuring and unconditional, three-fold promise: 1) Never again would floodwaters kill all living creatures. 2) As long as the earth remains, the seasons will always come as expected. 3) A rainbow will be visible when it rains as a sign to all that God will keep his promises." This covenant was between God and Noah as a representative of the human race, and took place in circa 3058 B.C.

That covenant was unconditional, but God also made clear certain requirements, including the penalty for taking another human life. Why was that? Because all people possess the qualities that distinguish them from animals: morality, reason, creativity, and self-worth. He then gave humankind a charge: "Be fruitful, multiply, and repopulate the earth."

After sometime, however, men, having become proud of their own accomplishments, said to each other, "Let us build a great city for ourselves with a tower that reaches the sky. This will make us famous." The tower itself was likely a huge ziggurat-configured structure, perhaps built on the plain between the Tigris and Euphrates Rivers. None of this, however, was in worship of God.

About all this it is recorded, the LORD said, "Come, let us (that is, Father, Son and Holy Spirit) go down and confuse the people with different languages. Then they won't be able to understand each other." In that way, the LORD scattered people all over the world.

Further, in the book of Acts we not only learn that He Himself gives all men life and breath and everything else, but that from one man He made every nation of men.

Since God created everything in the universe, it follows that if mankind should come to colonize other planets, they would then be no less beholden to God's Word and to the Lamb who has already given Himself up for sinners, whose eternal lives will be saved by grace. Let the story begin.

Terry Dodd

PART 1: DECISION ON JUN'OR

LIFT-OFF

One early morning on planet Jun'or in the year 2053 A.D., as its twin moons were receding from view, Son-tu felt a shiver of the same haunting memory that had gripped her every day for the past two weeks. It had also been her habit to journal for that same period. Two weeks prior had marked the thirty-year anniversary of her biological grandfather Gam'man's memorial funeral. Devastated at her loss at the time, she had remained on her grandfather's home planet for the next three decades, spending most of that time working as a Christian evangelist alongside her Jun'or-born husband, Boxxton, called "Boxx".

Some years earlier, upon being asked by a media interviewer as to whether she described herself as preacher or teacher, she confounded him with her answer: "I don't see myself as either, but rather someone who continuously reaches out from an evangelical and encourager's perspective. In short, even though some might think it quirky, I prefer to think of myself as a *reacher*."

She was indeed that, but she also sometimes referred to her non-profit organization as a "cutting edge" ministry. On the rare occasion when someone inquired about the "cutting edge" qualifier, she answered that she often had to resort to "cutting the edges" of expenses. Through Gam'man's and her own high profiles, however, she had been able to attract modest philanthropic support from both Earth and Jun'or for the ministry's evangelistic work.

This particular morning she was temporarily lost in a cocoon of remembrance of her first in-person meeting

15

with her grandfather. At the time, she had been grappling with a thirteen-year old's identity problem. Being a precocious young female novice in the Andivolean youth-training program was what had allowed her a coming-of-age test-journey for two weeks aboard a personal space craft.

She had been the only respondent to Gam'man's repetitious but compelling telepathic messages to "any unidentified aerial phenomenon pilot willing to meet with me, Gam'man, to answer any questions you might have concerning life outside of your own culture."

Because she had such a question, she responded, fully aware that by doing so she was putting herself at risk with her superiors. "Gam'man, do you know the Creator?" was her question.

She consented to clandestinely meet with him on the remote North Rim of the Grand Canyon. Their meeting was brief, but she shared something critical with the laid-back, fatherly person from Jun'or. Merely by making contact with an Earthling she risked her tentative Andivolean culture's standing. The revelation was no less than that she was the product of a one-time abducted Earthling and an Andivolian female donor's egg.

The well-read young woman at the time clearly remembered her emotional comment to Gam'man: "A true mother is someone who is more than an incubator. I have nothing to touch that belonged to my progenitors; no one to advise me about the secrets of life. Now, Gam'man, tell me of this 'kinsman redeemer' about whom it has been said has blotted out the sin of mankind."

Boxx interrupted Son-tu's vivid reverie, saying, "And for what new action-plan are you now laying foundations, my peripatetic wife?"

She looked up, her eyes still glistening from her fond recollection. She responded softy, "Listen, dear husband

Boxxton, I know you try not to utilize the Jun'orian curse of incidental telepathy reception, so what makes you believe I am thinking along any such specific line?"

She and Boxx had married not long after she immigrated with Gam'man to Jun'or. Boxx had been assigned to keep an eye on this supposedly controversial pair, given reports the local governing official had received from Earth. Even though he was acting in a specific official capacity he had quickly been won over due to the charm and sincerity of her character.

As for that first meeting's reaction to Boxx's compassionate inquiry, she could tell that although he appreciated the blessings of life, he, too, hungered for greater knowledge and truth.

As a part of their marriage vows he had volunteered a phrase Son-tu would never forget: "Whenever we leave one another, my thought will always be, 'Until we meet again.'"

"Well, dear," Boxx persisted, "since you are inquiring about the nature of my inquiry, I have long ago learned my lesson concerning your mental defenses against such telepathic efforts. Therefore, I can hardly claim to be able to read you like a book."

Son-tu blinked. "Wow! Now that's a fine one-liner. Who's writing your stuff these days?"

With a faux wrinkling of his forehead, he said, "Hey, I'm my own man! But back to my point, I'm merely wondering if you are harboring any latent inspirations as to changes in our static values."

"Well put!" she said with brightened eyes. "The answer is yes!"

Boxx sighed. "Then let me guess; are we to find ourselves space-bound aboard the long-pastured, hyper-leap ship *Boundless?*"

She laughed and said, "Unless you prefer to remain ground-bound."

He put up the palm of one hand. "In spite of my having asked, let me say I am not particularly enthusiastic about something as expansive as a planetary go-around. You know I prefer being a home-planet-body." He followed that with another sigh, this time more out of resignation than objection. "Would you . . . ah, mind sharing with me the essentials of the mission you have in mind?"

With a faux look of surprise on her face, she said, "You mean you really don't have a clue, given my many apparently too-subtle hints of late? Okay, there is more to what I am about to share with you, but a repetitive, confirming vision has come to me in recent weeks. Here it is: A spirit of sorts has appeared in my dreams, although I prefer the word 'vision.' It begins with this premise: Although energy is what powers life, it has no moral value."

She waited for two blinks of the eyes to see if that remark caused any reaction; zero. "Okay. The vision continues along this line: There is only one thing in the universe that has a true life's sense of worth and dignity, and that is humanity. Sadly, however, even though a sense of morality is inherent in all of mankind, individual possessors can, and do, deny it. This vision always concludes with something that seems to be saying, 'Obey your calling!'

"So, Master Boxx, with all of that supernatural imagery having been shared, here's the bottom line: I feel called to undertake a mission to reach people with the multiple messages of creationism, salvation, and a baby's right to life. In my opinion, sympathizers in opposition to these Christian issues are themselves shorn of supernaturalism and morality."

Boxx blanched and then exclaimed, "Now all of that is more than a mouthful! But I, too, know the only time we can put up treasures in heaven is before we die. So, when and where is this lonely evangelical couple mission-bound?"

"Oh, we aren't going by ourselves."

"Excuse me?"

"No. The Chessers are going with us. You've met Dr. Wy and his younger wife, Dr. Bea; both serving on Gam'man University's faculty."

"Well, first off, dear, you seem to have invited the Chessers before thee shared with me."

"Poetic; but no! I haven't yet invited them. That's why I mention them now, so that you will be more interested in the mission, my dear."

He scratched the back of his head and said, "When were you going to break the news to Jun'or's two busy leaders of the Rimerian Movement?"

She nodded absentmindedly and replied, "As soon as they arrive, which should be within the next half-hour."

RIMERIAN MOVEMENT LEADERS

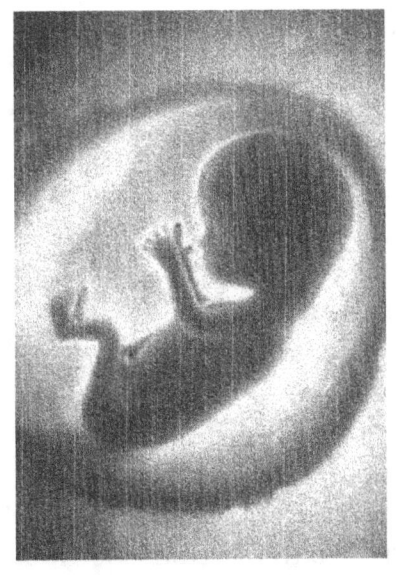

"Yet to be Delivered Citizen" from Sam Guzman's *Unborn Baby*, ProLife Wisconsin.org 2023, borrowed with permission from page 75 of R.B. Kuter's book, *The President's Bible*

At Son-tu's invitation the two Rimerian Movement leaders shortly found themselves gathering at Son-tu's and Boxx's residence for some unnamed announcement. "Absolutely not!" was Wy Chesser's response to Son-tu's proposition. At the same time, Wy put his arm around his wife as if to emphasize that the position's opposition was mutual.

Son-tu had long ago been primed by her grandfather as to why he had re-christened Chesser's son's name from the given adjective, "Young," to the proper noun, "Wy." Before the couple's arrival Son-tu shared that relevant circumstance with Boxx: The elder Chesser had been Gam'man's best friend before and after their mutual escape from incarceration on Jun'or's moon after each had been given significant sentences for their role in counterfeiting the national currency.

"It's actually quite simple," she said. "The nickname 'Wy' ('why' without pronouncing either the 'w' or the 'h') better defines *which* of the two Chessers."

"Okay, I get that," replied Boxx, "and as for Bea's given name, simply because I'm curious?"

"You might easily guess the answer to that."

"How so?"

Son-tu was having fun with this. "Okay, how would you describe her with a single word?"

He raised his eyes but didn't' hesitate before answering. "Beautiful," he said. "Oh, now I get that, too!"

"Hey, that was way too fast!"

"Yes. Probably so! Pitiful of me, wouldn't you say?"

Son-tu shrugged. "Hey, she is what she is."

(Narrator's note: Part of the reason we still don't live to God's mortality grant of the 120 years we read about in Genesis 6:3 is not due to design deficiency. It is because of the way humans have always treated their bodies.

However, this story has it that with time human society had acquired a combination of technological and medical skills necessary for common vital organ replacement; thus their longer mortality.)

Son-tu smoothly brushed aside Wy's previous verbal objection. "Come now, you two! This will be the extended vacation you have talked about, but never taken since your children went off to tertiary school and essentially abandoned you. I know you have planned well in terms of grooming your back-up; Johnni and Pyoter." She skipped several beats before continuing.

"And I can also share with you—Dr. Wy Chesser—that you will be afforded the opportunity to further edify to all willing to listen to at least scraps of your doctrinal thesis: "The Fable of Primitive Man's Time before Time was Recorded." I, too, will be anxious to echo much of the fascination of your argument."

With that, both Chessers turned to each other, their mouths still partially agape with surprise. But Son-tu hadn't finished her counter offer. "And as for you, Dr. Bea Chesser, get this: You will be our encyclopedic and doctrinal clarion crier against the yet popular curse of infanticide."

Bea was momentarily taken aback. "I am humbled to be branded with my conviction on that subject."

"Not at all, my good friend, for I too believe life begins at conception; partly because science proves that unborn babies can feel pain very early, and also that after only six weeks a baby's heartbeat can be heard in the womb. As you well know, sonograms show unborn babies smiling, yawning, and sucking their thumbs. I believe the first 3D ultrasound image of an unborn baby was demonstrated in 1986. But even more importantly, I place value in every human life, born and yet unborn."

21

Neither artificial nor natural light was at that moment needed to brighten the room as Bea tearfully said, "When do we leave? But I think we first need to check in with the Board Chairman for such an extensive travelogue. As for the GU President, we needn't be concerned. I think he may be up for an unscheduled retirement."

Son-tu replied, "Uh, I have already approached Chairman Washington for the favor of your temporary hiatus. He was excited about the mission itself and blessed your participation, should you decide to accept."

That led to the near simultaneous response from the pair; "We're in!"

"Wait a minute!" Boxx barked. "What am *I* . . . the luggage bearer?"

"Of course not, honey. In addition to contributing to the aforementioned talking points, you, as always, are navigator and gunner."

He sighed, saluted, and said, "Aye, Captain: ballasts aweigh!"

PART II: JOURNEY TO ANDIVOLI

MISSION LAUNCH

The Jun'or foursome had been aboard *Boundless's* relatively small but adequate five-compartment/four-person craft for ten days. It was so-named for its ever-dependable gravity-driven power source. The crew had just emerged from the hyper jump when Son-tu said to Boxx, "First Officer, locate the nearest orbital service station for permission to enter Andivoli's space. I understand they have a new procedure for global entry."

"Will do, Captain," he said with a faux left-handed salute, his right hand being engaged with a combination of onboard computer manipulations and his com-glasses.

Son-tu gave him a faux frown in return. "I will overlook the borderline insubordinate response, but you do know the Andivoleans don't favor unofficial visitors from either Jun'or or Earth."

"So I've read," he replied, pausing for a moment in mentally recognizing the magnitude of their next step. That occasioned him to make some comments about the current state of human versus robotic communications while at the same time monitoring the ship's dashboard. "It still amazes me that human technology has at long last allowed us to become un-shackled from having to look down at yester-decades' small, hand-held cell phone, or even sitting in a stationery spot while interacting through a wireless keyboard on a desk or a wall."

He shook his head as if in wonder and continued, "Augmented reality has changed the entire paradigm. Now we are able to have a heads-up view of the physical world and to interact through digital content with useful tools

embedded in a three-dimensional, com-glass headset like this one."

"That was profound commentary, dear, but you are correct in that 'heads-up' is a good plan for whatever God allows to be sent our way. As a matter of fact, now that I think about it, my name may well be listed on some Andivolean chart as a no-favor entity, merely for my one-time attribution of their decades-long harassment-craft being satanically-influenced."

At that, she felt the need to further support her statement, even if it was only for the other three's benefit. "The greatest trick Satan has ever pulled was convincing the world that he doesn't exist. No one can extinguish Almighty God's everlasting light; least of all Satan, with all his empty promises."

She wasn't quite finished with her observations about Andivoli: "The democratic idea remains vivid for mankind, yet for decades upon decades hundreds of thousands of people—sometimes millions—leave poor, violent and poorly governed countries in search of a better life. Their destination-of-choice has never been autocratic. And in terms of a literal brave new world, it would not be the colonized Andivolean planet. Why not? Its ministers prefer well-regulated regions. But again, because of the arc of history I believe that is the very thing which makes Andivoli a field ripe for the Christian harvest."

Boxx rubbed his chin. "Now that is a litany worth recording. I am sorry to hear it end, *Captain Son-tu*, but our computer adjustments for orbital holding are complete. I have one relevant question: How shall we present ourselves in terms of our purpose for visiting Andivoli?"

Wy interrupted. "I've been thinking about that very thing. We might try a reverse approach."

"Reverse?" Boxx questioned the professor.

"Well, since there has always existed an unreasonable hostility directed toward Christians, suppose we stroke this Andivolean interviewer by claiming to be a team from something called the Galactic Historical Society, wanting to re-ascribe credit to Andivoli for its colonial heroes."

Son-tu offered a minimal frown, but also nodded. "Hm'm, my good Dr. Chesser, I don't know how Christian is a *little* deception, but if it gets us down for the beginning of our Mission to Mankind, I'm good. Let's try it. Bea, in case papers might be needed for the gatekeepers, would you prepare some appropriate-appearing papers in case our opening bid is called?"

Boxx gave Son-tu a thumbs up, but added, "There's no great rush. We're in the queue, but it will still take us almost 24 hours to dock. Andivoli is the Queen Planet of Inefficiency."

As Bea and Wy sat in their semi-rigid hammocks in their cubicle's quarters, she said to her husband, "That's *their* story for the inter-planetary interviewer once we dock. What's *our* story?"

"Yes. We might as well be prepared for that possibility as well." He looked upward for a moment before nabbing an invisible something from the air. "Since we're playing 'what if,' we could try this: 'Earth scientists have concluded there is no such thing as pre-historic time, and my wife and I will be making such a presentation on that subject to the General Andivolean Council."

It was Bea's turn to frown. In an attempt to land the out-of-control trivia game she said, "Do you really think anyone in such a minor position as this would likely be qualified to pursue such a tactic? Look, if anyone appears to be touting outsized authority, just point out our leader's Andivolean citizenship."

Nearly a day later it was a fuzzily-imaged Andivolean gate-keeper seated at a monitor who intoned, "Madam Son-tu, I am afraid your personal papers are not in order." Continuing in an obviously disinterested monotone, he added, "They do not reflect authorization for more than one accompanying attendee. Which of your party will be exiting upon landing?"

Son-tu turned to the others with a look of surprise and whispered, "It's a robot!"

"What?" was Wy's muffled aside.

Son-tu turned away from the monitor and said—still with low tones—"I've read about Andivolian policies increasingly employing robotic labor in order to compensate for low planetary reproductive genetics, but this . . ."

Wy shook his head while continuing to whisper. "This is pathetic! Significant robotic replacement of the human workforce is a losing proposition. We tried it on Jun'or decades ago. It is readily arguable that a society's dependence upon robots ultimately begets a soft and decadent society. Even Earth's famed science fiction writer Isaac Asimov once described such a society's resultant robotic technology as necessarily dwindling and dying out of sheer boredom and lack of motivation."

Frowning had apparently become contagious as Son-tu settled things in saying, "Well, that may be, but it is also the technology which is denying our admittance. I think we'll just play this by ear."

Addressing the interviewer an hour later, Son-tu said, "Sir or Madam, you see by my papers that I am a dual citizen of Jun'or and Andivoli. It is required that human citizens and their party be given clearance to present any petition before the people's representative."

"Pardon me, ma'am, the gender reference to a robot is 'citizen.' If you prefer a proper name, however, mine is

Mechanix." Out of apparent pride, it added, "I named my-self."

At that, Son-tu blinked and said, "I did not realize there would be a need of robotic gender ID, but thank you for sharing your name. Now, I either require clearance for exiting the terminal or the opportunity to speak to your human supervisor."

"I am not aware of that requirement distinctive, ma'am, but lacking a human supervisor at this facility your entourage is reluctantly granted progressive admittance to Andivoli. Please check your arrival status at the indicated physical coordinates. Should you return at another instance, however, we will be better prepared to deal with your argument." Then, with what could pass as a robotic smirk, it added, "May you spend many credits but little time on Andivoli."

Son-tu turned to the others and said, "What do you know? A robotic stand-up comic!"

NOT A HOMECOMING CROWD

Docking at the "Temporary Space Traveler Terminal," the four-person crew quickly disembarked. Addressing a receptionist at a counter marked, "Passports", Son-tu courteously reported as "Captain of the Jun'or-registered *Boundless*, requesting Andivoli passports for four."

The robot checked its screen and responded in a monotone, minus any obvious eye contact, "Four *provisional* passports are hereby issued, Captain Son-tu."

"What is the nature of the *provision*?" Son-tu asked.

"Provided that your visit is not shortened."

"And what might be the cause of our visit being 'shortened'?"

"That would be defined as tenure's end, i.e., should anyone of your party say or do anything reported as being anti-Andivolean. Next applicant!"

Shortly after having also registered at one of the spaceport's several hospitality traveler facilities, they proceeded via robotic air taxi to the nearest so-named Public Address Center. Boxx rhetorically commented to the other three, "Are we meant to evangelize a robotic society?"

Son-tu laughed and said, "No, only non-robotic Andivoleans are tuned to the address center's microwave broadcast emitter. It is hardly aimed at gratuitous messaging, however. This system is a double-pronged communications tool. In addition to general local information and advertising, it is also a governmental revenue-producer. Its first payers are the message bearers, the second payers are the subscribers. For every real-time public news bite delivered, three sight-and-sound commercial ads or government propaganda bites are accommodated. Oh; there is zero muting option."

Bea contributed a laugh and added, "You mean other than disconnection! What other electronic recreation resource does a robotic-oriented society have for the business of the local human population's benefit?"

"Let me guess," said Wy. "Since social media is not a part of this society, we have another zero."

Son-tu sighed. "But since we are not allowed to circulate among the general population, *this* is what is available to us."

Boxx threw up the obvious question: "Do we have any idea as to the percentage of Andivoleans who are believers?"

"Yes," was the response from the one Andivolean of the group. "While it is not zero, neither is it a double-digit percentage. We have, however, a specific target category;

28

those rebels who might either actively yearn for a degree of freedom from an essentially robotic government, or those whose conscience has been pricked by the Creator, as was the case at one time for each of the four of us."

CENTRAL-COM STATION

The foursome regrouped at the entrepreneurial station center to which they were directed. They were surprisingly greeted, not robotically, but by a human operations clerk.

"Greetings, visitors from Jun'or," he began. "Are you inquiring about buying some audio and visual time for perhaps some of your planet's famous artificial nuts, bananas, or other?"

"Thank you, citizen—uh—what is your name, please?"

"Oh, pardon the omission. The name is Gollier-ta."

"Son-tu's eyebrows raised. "Again, we thank you. Well, yes, broadcast time is indeed what we are after." With little forethought, she jokingly added, "And yes, we have no bananas."

"Gollier-ta's eyes narrowed as he said, "We may not be as provincial as you think. What is the nature of your business?"

Son-tu recognized her insensitivity, perhaps brought on by the orbital station robot's remarks. "Please accept my apology for the indiscretion, Gollier-ta. What are your rates?"

"Apology accepted. Are any of you Andivolean?"

"That would be me. So-tu is my given name, after the Andivolean human custom of the hyphenated "tu" for female, and "ta" for males." She then added, "The addendum is for the benefit of my traveling companions."

Their guide nodded. "Excuse my hesitation. Few Andivoleans travel off-planet. Welcome indeed. As to rates for other-planet visitors, I am sorry to say they are twice the rate as for local organizations and individuals, but they are nevertheless a bargain, given the system's strong circulation."

Son-tu was amused. "That is a quaint descriptor for an electronic medium."

"Sorry, it is my own choice. I'm a writer by preference, but such a hobby doesn't pay enough to even circulate heat in my flat."

Son-tu again found herself momentarily distracted. "You know, you are the second comedian we have encountered on this trip. The other was a robot, but its remark was out of sarcasm. I like your personality."

At that, the other three of the crew each frowned, with Boxx saying in a fatherly-like, but joking sense, "Well, my dear, you seem to be straying from the task at hand; perhaps due to space lag."

Gollier-ta looked around, as if to be certain his supervisor might not have overheard the conversation. "Visitors, I, too apologize. I have more than once been chastised for my sometime curious welcoming perspective. Although my conscience requires of me a degree of transparency, it does not always contribute to my commissions."

Having recovered from the conversation's diversion, Son-tu re-focused. "Not at all. I find your banter refreshing. So what do we receive for such 'bargain' rates, Gollier-ta?"

"Thank you for your interest! A full seven-day week's coverage includes five full minutes every four hours during daylight. I recommend a schedule of 8-12-4-8, payable in Andivolean national currency. For a small fee we can also accommodate your currency exchange."

Wy raised a hand in saying, "Pardon me, but I have two questions. What is the typical broadcast recipient's reception method, and is there a discount for a second consecutive week of delivery?"

The agent responded eagerly. "The receiving appliance is primarily that of com-glasses, but some stationary appliances also come into play. As for an additional time-slot purchase option, yes, that is available. And it would earn you a slight discount. When would you care to begin?"

Settled in at their austere, but doable accommodations, Son-tu opened discussion with the other three. "The operative word for the message aspect is *brevity*. If we can't deliver the desired message in a short time for each airing, then we will have accomplished nothing. Folks aren't going to tune in for a speech from an unknown entity, much less for a repeat treatment."

"What do you mean?" asked Bea with a frown. "We speak truth."

"Speaking too much truth to power in any society is dangerous, much more so in a controlled state. To begin, I suggest three-minute blurbs on alternating days directed to salvation and creationism, followed by a one-minute blurb on an unborn human baby's right to life."

Wy responded with, "Done! We obviously need repetition of each day's message if we are to reach a reasonable number of the human population. I propose we go with the manager's suggested schedule and repeat each morning's recording the other three times each day."

Son-tu was agreeable. "Would all three of you please give me some scripts of not more than 125 words per minute?"

"I have a question," said Boxx, whose tightened lips betrayed the nature of what he was about to say. "What concerns should we have about censorship from the station and possible negative feedback from callers?"

Son-tu thought for a moment before answering. "That will fall to me to manage at the time."

DAY ONE BROADCAST

"Greetings, Andivoleans, from your neighboring planet Jun'or. My name is Son-tu, and I am a citizen of Andivoli. At this same time over the balance of this week I will be bringing you God's Word as to the many wonders wrought for your benefit. Do not hesitate to feed back to this central station any questions specific to salvation, creationism or infanticide. If they are relevant, I will be happy to address a few of them on-air.

"I once believed, as many of you, that both we and our world are the result of naturalism over millions of years. But when as a young person I came to marvel at the birth of life, the order of the heavens, and even the very design of nature, I began to wonder if it didn't make more sense for there to be a designer, rather than the random chance of sustainable human, animal and plant life through evolution. In other words, apart from supernatural creation, the incredible order we daily observe makes no sense.

"Think about this colonized planet we call Andivoli. As with Earth, its atmosphere has the perfect mix of oxygen and nitrogen for human, animal and plant life. In the natural state—at least so far as we know—no such atmospheres exist anywhere but on Earth, Jun'or and Andivoli. Such complex elements could not collectively evolve. As for human life, it has only developed once—on Earth. As for the two other inhabitable planets in this galaxy, colonists from Earth brought human life and technology with them.

"Evolutionist thinking further states that there must have been a time before the beginning of recorded history when human beings were so primitive that, although they could remember events, they could not communicate through speech. According to that false theory, speech was invented, allowing people to express memories and to transfer them across time from generation to generation. That is hardly fact, however, as recorded through early history's only observable witness, its Author and Almighty Creator.

"Dear fellow humans, in this galaxy it is our stable sun that is so necessary for living things. And that, too, is part of God's design for us. Now, bear with me a further minute as I pose a few critical remarks concerning an equally important subject about which this world, Jun'or, and Earth have all seen its share.

"There is something the average person can do to dampen infanticide, the single greatest atrocity ever inflicted upon humankind. You know it as abortion, but that word is intended to be callously dismissive of the unstated expectation of a fetus in escaping the womb with his or her life, just as had been granted the unborn infant's mother. If you have never given this serious thought, I ask you to do so at this time.

"That is all the time I have been allotted for this message, but there is much more to come. Please tune in at this same time tomorrow. This is Son-tu of Andivoli saying, 'until tomorrow.'"

FOLLOWING THE FIRST DAY

That evening, following the last of the day's three repeated broadcasts, Wy addressed the mission's next day's message. "Thank you for the excellent kick-off, Son-tu. I think we are all anxious to see the initial reaction to our first day's efforts, including the station's response. We should get the first real sense of that early tomorrow." After a moment's pause, he added, "Do you think we are likely to be given the hook by station management?"

Son-tu shook her head, saying, "I don't think that will happen, at least not soon. Remember that although this station is government-licensed, it is not government-run, nor is it a not-for-profit. It's in business to make money. And in order to make a profit, it needs advertisers. Advertisers only get exposure if people tune in, and information, entertainment and controversy are what create an audience."

DAY TWO

"Good morning, Andivoli!" Son-tu began. "When I introduced myself to you yesterday I invoked the name of God, about whom everyone knows, but with whom few actually have a personal relationship. Some of you accept that truth while others do not, and still others consider the statement an affront. Merely reading from the Creator's (Owner's) manual—the Holy Bible, which the first colonists brought with them as a part of the colonial culture exported from Earth—however, does not make one right with God.

"Neither does simply obeying civil or criminal law make us right with God. Even the Jewish Laws of Moses' time could not *save* a person. In fact, the purpose of the Law in Jesus's time—and long before and after—was to humble people and drive them to repentance and faith in Jesus the Christ, the Messiah (John 7:19-20).

"But why do people who *instinctively* obey the law do so? It is written in everyone's heart! Your own conscience and thoughts either accuse you or tell you that you are doing right. You will certainly find this truth in your Bible (Romans 2:13-16). Its verses close with this proclamation:

'The day is coming when the Creator and Savior God, through Christ Jesus, will judge everyone's secret life.'

"What is the solution to avoiding the delusions of a world and its eternal damnation for having rebelled against God the Creator? We all know that the older we grow, the dimmer the faculties of hearing and seeing become. In the same way, our capacity to hear the voice of God diminishes with age. One of time's most venerated preachers has given us these wise words: 'There are many who are deceived by Satan into thinking that there is plenty of time to get right with God.' But I ask you, will tomorrow really be better than today?' That is a delusion that can cause one to be finally and eternally lost. I will have more to share on this point tomorrow.

"Switching subjects before closing today's message, recall that during yesterday's broadcast I introduced the subject of the single greatest human atrocity in history, which is abortion. And because this term is much more appropriately named for the abomination it is, I label it as infanticide. Yes, the woman who has an abortion is a murderess. I know that's a strong statement, but so is the murder of an unborn baby.

"As one fervent defender of an unborn baby's right to life has put it, 'When any plant-seed is germinated and begins the process of growth it is considered to have *life*. How much more viable and miraculous is the *life* of the fertilized human egg *living* within the womb of a woman?' And yet, people everywhere have been divided on this issue for decade upon decade; century upon century. Fortunately, some nations have appropriately come to place its legality in the hands of voters in individual states, provinces or regions. Ponder this perspective. This is Sontu saying, 'until tomorrow.'"

Just before the end of the second day's broadcasts, a call came in from someone whose interest had obviously been piqued by the message. Boxx was screening and immediately passed him onto Son-tu. "My name is Bing-ta, and my question has to do with the specific *order* of space, time, and matter having been 'created' in the universe."

Son-tu's response: "That, sir, is an unanticipated, but excellent question. God surely created all three at the same time. Why do I say that? If there were matter, but no space, *where* would you put matter? And if there were matter and space, but no time, *when* would you put them?"

To that, the caller waited three or four beats before responding, but then with a curious comment. "You have answered my question thoughtfully. I have a special reason to appreciate that. I hope to call in again."

Afterward, Son-tu asked the crew what they thought of the final caller's question. Bea quickly spoke up. "Well, speaking of the *miraculous* nature of God's having simultaneously created space, matter, and time, I nevertheless put that fellow's interesting trifecta second in importance compared to the conception of human life."

Boxx, sniffing opportunity, introduced a differing comment. "*Second?*" he said.

"Yes, second!"

Boxx persisted. "Pardon me, 'Judge', but I will concede you a fine Silver Medal, but not the Gold Medal in a comparison with ultimate creation."

Son-tu and Wy looked at each other with expressions of *What do we have here, boys and girls?*"

Wy took on the position of referee. "Okay, you two. Let's have a clean conversation here."

Boxx chose to remain on his high-horse perspective and unthinkingly responded to Wy with, "What wisdom wouldst thou care to impart to the younger generation?"

It was not lost on Son-tu that, intended or not, Boxx had just made an implied reference to Wy's 15-year greater age than Bea's and his. "Boxx!" Son-tu called him out. "Has hyper jet lag caused you to take leave of your sense of civility?"

Instantly feeling correctly chastised, Boxx retreated. Turning to face the Chessers he said, "I apologize to both of you. I guess that any form of denial of the Christian foundational nature of creationism is, at least in my mind, a sin of either omission or commission. Forgive my remark, although intended in jest, it was nevertheless inappropriate."

"Apology accepted," Bea sincerely offered as she first glanced at Wy and then to Boxx. "We should always agree to disagree on nonessential Christian points."

Son-tu had yet to weigh in on her own question but preceded it. "Thank you all for your observations, but frankly I was impressed by the caller for yet another reason: He not only spoke well and thoughtfully, but he also understands the value of white space in speaking."

CHANGING THE COURSE OF HUMANITY

"Listeners and viewers," Son-tu began the third day's broadcast, "after yesterday's session my crew had an interesting and hypothetical discussion about whether creationism or an unborn baby's right-to-life deserved the greater medal in terms of critical importance for humanity. I come to you today with yet a different perspective.

"Among all the forces that have shaped humanity, certainly the story of Jesus ranks as the most powerful in terms of eternity. Since it first began to be told in the *day*—perhaps hours—following Jesus' sacrificial death on the cross in Jerusalem on Earth in *the year of the Lord* (1 A.D.), it has wielded influence impossible to calculate.

"The story has shaped the entire course of Christianity and its understanding of the world and of the Creator God. The telling of the story was an enterprise of Christian believers long before anyone thought of themselves as Christians. It began after Jesus' resurrection when one of his followers was asked to explain to an unrecognizable questioner (Jesus) just who this Person was and why His followers had not disbanded.

"His ministry, death, and resurrection set off a chain reaction of proclamation and interpretation of His life that quickly elevated His story from obscurity to cosmic significance. It has never stopped. It is not only the single most important thing in *this* life, but also in the eternal life to come.' A pause of two beats ensued. "Until tomorrow, this is Son-tu of Andivoli."

BING-GO

Days three and four went as planned with additional illuminations being provided each day concerning salvation's case for Christ, foundational creationism, and abhorrent infanticide. At literally the end of the day's live broadcast, the same caller from a few days earlier surprised Son-tu. Once again, screener Boxx quickly switched his call to her.

"This is Bing-ta again. I have reason to ask another question. Why do you insist upon bucking the overwhelming mainstream cadre of scientists' conviction for millions of years of evolution?"

"Thank you for your call-back, Bing-ta. Now, because you have raised a fundamental and legitimate question which is likely on the minds of many, I am going to invoke an option I earlier negotiated with this station. With your permission, a special response is going to be inserted ahead of the next scheduled program. I will address your question live and beginning now. Are you okay with that?"

The caller not only had no objection, but said, "I welcome it."

"Thank you, Bing-ta. To bring our audience up to speed, a last-minute caller has just asked a fundamental question about creationism. In response to that we are extending this broadcast to address his well-stated question, which is this: 'Why do I, Son-tu, insist upon bucking the overwhelming mainstream cadre of scientists' convictions for millions of years of evolution?' Here is my response: First of all, Jesus, the Christ, came to humanity as a lamb, sacrificed Himself for us on the cross, was resurrected and seen by some 500 witnesses . . . but one day he will return as a lion. In the meantime, his believers are charged not merely with defending their position, but charging the opposition.

"That said, it is granted that the case for the origin of life via chemical evolution—as usually presented—not only sounds plausible but has been widely accepted. I will add to that by saying popularizations have also carried the case to millions in a persuasive manner. Now, even though the fact of chemical evolution cannot be satisfactorily falsified, its apparent plausibility can nevertheless be exaggerated. Thus, it tends to move beyond its true status as speculation to be regarded instead as knowledge.

"Much closer to the true fact, however, is that reasonable doubts exist in the general scientific community concerning whether simple chemicals on a primitive Earth did or could spontaneously evolve (i.e., organize themselves) into the first life. Let me add to this that circumstantial evidence is as often a liar as it sometimes is of truth. How is that? Facts themselves are meaningless. It's only the interpretation we give those facts which count."

She paused a moment with the added hint of a smile before satisfying a whimsical urge. "Allow me to fancifully close on the aspect of circumstantial evidence: Earth's ancient entertainment archives tell us that this point was clearly made for the audience of the one-time popular television-watching public in an attorney-character's episode titled *The Case of the Perjured Parrot.* I will leave it to your imagination as to how the word 'perjury' in that segment might have played out.

"But I digress. Caller Bing-ta, if I may ask, what sort of work do you do?"

"My business stinks!" he said, then laughing before qualifying his statement. "I run several fish-processing plants on Andivoli's largest man-made lake."

"So you are a fisherman?" Son-tu said, hoping that the relevant occupation of the disciples was not lost on him.

"That is an interesting term for me," he replied. "I have never thought of myself as a fisherman, although from a biblical perspective I have no objection. Fishery management, however, doesn't occupy all of my time."

Now those are a couple of interesting statements, she thought, but decided to hold off pursuing her own question. "Thank you, sir. Now, further as to your question about this great majority of scientists you say have thrown in with the theory of millions of years of natural evolution, I doubt many of them are actually convinced of the *theory.* I am obviously a dissenter, but the fact is that for the most part, dissenting *arguments* from mainstream science have always been generally negative and *for* the supernatural creationism view. If that sounds convoluted, allow me to share a few more things with this audience:

"Six thousand years ago, a civilization arose unlike any the world had ever seen before. In particular support of this Biblical history there is an extraordinary scientific research publication from many years back called the Jeanson Correlation. This was authored by Dr. Nathan Jeanson, and involves extensive Y chromosome Adam/Noah and DNA claims that the history of civilization spans only 4,500 years. That would take us back to the worldwide flood of Noah's time and a total of only between 6,000 and 10,000 years. In accordance with that, the DNA of ancestors of record traces mankind's history back to the first man, Adam.

"Now follow me: Science thus denies that human history reaches back 200,000 or more years of evolution's claims; and in the same breath it is also denying the longer timescale associated with this view. So, if God created Adam 6,000 years ago on the sixth day of creation—and He *did*—then the DNA implication is that the universe is only six to ten thousand years old as well.

"What is the even greater implication of this? If human history is only of that age, and if the universe is also only a few thousand years older, then humans certainly did *not* evolve from ape-like creatures. And wholesale evolution of all species must also be out of the question. As an obviously relevant aside we should ask, 'How can both apes and humans simultaneously exist?'

"Now, dear listeners and viewers, to the facts of these well-documented scientific claims, let me pose a hypothetical question: If God's crown achievement is mankind—which is clearly stated in the Owner's manual, i.e., the Holy Bible—for what possible reason would He have created life millions of years *before* mankind—the Creator's avowed crown jewel?"

Bing-ta, the program's caller, replied. "Your explanation is much more on point than what I expected. I am impressed and pleased, but I cannot put my many thoughts and words in order at this time. May I be excused?"

Son-tu downplayed her keen interest in the caller's engaging questions and comments by responding with, "Certainly! Thank you so much for initiating this interchange, Bing-ta. I look to hear from you again."

PRIOR TO DAY SIX'S BROADCAST

No sooner had Son-tu and her crew arrived at the station early the following morning but what the station manager met them. His hands were clasped as he exclaimed, "What an amazing interchange! All of our incoming lines were tied up for two hours last night following responses to your impromptu broadcast."

Wy asked the obvious question. "Is that a plus or a minus?"

"Positive or negative reaction is irrelevant to me! Either way makes for a plus for this station. As it has always been, legitimate controversy is king with electronic media. As for the crew from *Boundless*, I would call it break-even. Half were for you and half against. Now, what's up for day six?"

Son-tu couldn't let pass the opportunity just presented. "By 'day six,' kind sir, are you referring to creation or to our broadcasts?" The analogy was either too subtle or simply irrelevant for its intended recipient and brought no reaction other than a brief frown. She continued, undaunted. "Okay, tomorrow's message will involve the key element of part two of the Owner's manual; that which is latent throughout part one: salvation through Christ."

She qualified the agenda even further. "Gollier-ta, permit me to ask of you a question which I will be putting to my audience: What is the meaning of these six words from the Holy Bible, *"O death, where is thy sting?"*

He cocked his head and said without serious interest, "I honestly do not know, but my first thought is that it is probably found in one of William Shakespeare's plays."

"You are correct, but only because old Will borrowed it from the Holy Bible; 1st Corinthians 15:55. More importantly, what is its meaning?"

The manager shook his head. "I will not attempt to show myself more clueless than I fear I already have."

Son-tu did not expect more, and proceeded to answer her own question: "Twelve words in John 3:16 make it very clear: *"Everyone who believes in him (Jesus Christ) will never perish, but have eternal life.* How can both be true? I mean, isn't dead, dead? That's the subject for tomorrow's broadcast."

"All I can say, Madam Son-tu, is that you know how to stir the kettle. Have at it all the more . . . but be very careful. What you share with me is one thing, but through this station *might* be another."

THE NEXT TWO DAY'S BROADCASTS

Relative to the previous day, things were quiet for the sixth day's live broadcast. Son-tu continued to make a strong supporting case for salvation through the sinless Christ-man Jesus having come down from paradise for the sole purpose of sacrificing Himself for the evil heart possessed by every newborn member of humankind. She followed that up with the equally strong case for creationism vs. evolution and closed with a shorter segment against the collective cultural ethos of infanticide and its resultant nightmarish human cost to any such society.

Prior to that day's final recorded broadcast the station manager sought out Son-tu at the station. He enthusiastically queried about a second week's airtime contract. She demurred with a formal statement, "If it pleases you, we will make the call after assessing tomorrow's actual broadcast completion."

As the seventh and final day's planned evangelistic segment was wrapping up, a by-now familiar caller made his third call. Screener Boxx quickly patched him in to Son-tu. The caller commenced speaking without bothering to identify himself: "I once piloted a similar craft as yours, Madam Son-tu. In fact, it was during the same time-frame as your seventh inning of the confrontation these many years ago on Earth, but I was working as a sort of free-lance reporter. When I subsequently shared with my supervisor about the message of your public coming out, I was immediately sent back to Andivoli and prosecuted for having challenged Andivolean interests."

She immediately recognized the caller's name, saying, "From the sound of your voice, Bing-ta, I welcome you back, but you have shocked me with your announcement."

"Yes, thank you. Sorry to catch you unawares. May we talk?"

Since she only had seconds before going off the air she decided to react more pro-actively. "Would you care to meet with me in person?"

"Thank you. That is why I have called."

"Can you manage mid-afternoon tomorrow at my crew's quarters? My producer-screener will give you the address."

"I can."

Following the minutes-later conclusion of the final day's broadcast contract, the station manager said to Son-tu in the same formal tone as he had used the day before. "I reminded you, ma'am, about being circumspect as to your subjects. Creationism, salvation and an un-born baby's right to life are of one faith nature, but intimation of governmental criticism of Andivoli, is quite another. It would not surprise me if we—that is, you *and* I—may shortly be the recipients of some Andivolean agency's visit."

"Don't worry, Gollier-ta. Mention of that incident on Earth by a program caller had to do with ancient history. In any event, I will certainly clear you of any suspected complicity in such an incidental call-in. I do not think, however, that we will need a second week for program-ming. Thank you for your help, sir."

MISSION FOCUS EXPANDED

That afternoon, Son-tu welcomed Bing-ta into their traveler-visitation facility's modest common area. The two shook hands and sat down. She spoke first. "I am curious about three things; first, do you have anything else to share about your coincidental connection with my time on Earth? Then, if you would, speak to me concerning your closing comment about hoping I would ask to meet with you in-person. The other item would have to do with your statement about your fishery business not occupy-ing all of your time."

"Thank you, but if I may, I would prefer deferring my answers to those questions until we have talked a bit more."

That is odd, but not objectionable, she thought, but since neither of them could read the other's thoughts, she said, "Okay, what would you like to talk about?"

"You! What is on your mind?"

"On my mind?" she frowned in repeating his question. *Now, this fellow is on my mind.*

45

"Yes," the visitor said, nodding. "What are you about? Who is Son-tu?"

My goodness, she thought. *When was the last time I've been asked that question?*

"You obviously know some of it, but your question causes me to think back to my early teens when I was something of a prodigy caught up in the Andivolean far left culture in which I had been raised. That earlier time was when I sensed the mind of my unknowing Jun'orian biological grandfather Gam'man. He was residing on Earth after having many decades earlier escaped imprisonment for a petty crime committed by he and his close friend and a third—let me say—evil-genius colleague."

She paused several beats before continuing, not certain as to how deeply she wanted to dig into the dirt of her past in satisfying this stranger's curiosity. "Gam'man managed to reach Earth. Unfortunately, it was his rebellious, bastard son who would find himself as the innocent abductee-father. He passed not long after the abduction, but not before the result of his sperm having been brought to fruition with an Andivolean female donor's egg. But to conclude the story, friend Bing-ta, I utilized mental telepathy in responding to Gam'man's telepathic search for a possible maverick Andivolean pilot of a UFO. My big question for Gam'man at that time was, 'Do you know the Creator?'"

Bing-ta was impressed. "That was bold! And did he?"

"No. He said he did, but I understood that he did not. I believe God used me to prick my grandfather's conscience. And out of that situation both of us would come to know Him. It is thus my personal relationship with the Creator that has come to inspire and guide me every minute of my life.

"That is my story. Now, sir, if you could tell me what has happened to you in the years since having been reproved by Andivolean planetary harassers?" She hesitated a moment before letting her voice drop before adding, "And whatever your story, I am intrigued by what prompts your obviously entrepreneurial efforts within such a divisive robotic culture as this."

The visitor's eyes brightened. "Thank you! I am not only satisfied, but appreciative. I, too, might add that you have just offered me the opportunity to segue. Allow me to first comment on your last remark. I once read a remarkable quote from nearly a half-century ago by Henry Louis Gates, Jr. concerning Earth's Western civilization. I liked it so much that I took it to fit with my Christian perspective. It goes like this: 'We transcend division by recognizing that any human being sufficiently curious and motivated can fully possess another culture, no matter how 'alien' it may appear to be.'

"Okay," he said, "that is introductory. Now you want to hear my personal story. After my otherwise innocent, but outrageously-deemed cultural criticism I was sentenced to five years of governmental robotics repair. Through that, I was fortuitously provided with an avenue of survival. I was able to capitalize by absorbing the technology which was essentially dropped into my lap.

"From that point I began melding my new life with a combination of inborn curiosity and creative imagination. I believe the Creator pricked my conscience, just as He had yours and your grandfather's. As a result, I revolted against the pagan Andivolean culture and got my hands on a copy of the Holy Bible."

"Fascinating," she said while folding her hands, thereby encouraging him to share more.

"What you may find difficult to believe," he continued, "is that I, too, am a biologic product of an abducted Earth male and an Andivolean female's donor egg. But," he quickly added, "my abductee sperm donor was not a Jun'orian."

Son- tu was further shocked, but knew she needed to drill down. "Okay, my friend, it is time for you to put the rest of your cards onto the table. Is there anything else you would like to share before you tell me what we can do for you, or vice versa?"

She had just pre-empted his launch into the answer to that very question, which caused him to smile. "Thank you for that grace. What else am I about? Well, after my break with the government I married a fine woman, whom I lost to the never-ending universal dread of cancer. It was actually she who led me to listen to the Creator's call to surrender to Him." With that emotional admission he stiffened his upper lip before moving on to the next part of his story.

"I think I understand the focus of your interest, Son-tu. Because I am a rare Andivolean believer, I simply welcomed your initial broadcasts. However, I could barely believe my eyes and ears at your candid statements concerning your evangelistic fervor for the people of Andivoli. Out of that I have another question I would now like to pose. Your answer to it might have a bearing on each of our futures."

Now that is not something a person hears every day, nor wants to. This had better be good!

DISCIPLESHIP IN A CAN

"Here is my question," Bing-ta began. "What is your greatest concern for people once they have made a decision to accept Christ?"

Her raised eyebrows betrayed her reaction to his question. "That, my friend, is the single most important question for any Christian evangelist. How do we see to the discipleship—or mentoring—of a new Christian?"

"That is precisely my point!" he said with conviction. "Salvation is but a start towards living a Christian life. Others have noted that graduation from anything is not the end but the beginning. But does that truly apply to faith in the Christ?"

With a smile and a brief nod of her head Son-tu acknowledged yet another good question by her erudite new acquaintance. "Allow me to illustrate my perspective on that," she said. "After I had spoken to you electronically for the first time, I knew *of* you. Now that we have met in person, however, I have become *acquainted* with you. But not until I have the opportunity to spend significant time with you will I actually *know* you. Only then will I have a *personal relationship* with you. Are we on the same page?"

Bing-ta's broad smile was accompanied by five words: "Behold, the light cometh on."

She wasn't certain as to whether that comment was about her or him. Ignoring it, she replied, "Correct! Only when a person has a personal relationship with the Creator does he or she have the basis for spiritual growth with our LORD and Savior. And how does that develop, but with immersion into the Word, with repetition."

With a curt nod of the head, he replied, "Not only do I fully understand, but I believe I have a solution to the problem!"

Really? was her reaction in thought. She knew all the standard, but less than efficacious solutions to the age-old Christian paradox, so she was inclined to doubt he had anything to offer beyond the following: 1) Providing the new convert either with appropriate literature or access to it, 2) Recommending him or her to begin attending a church of their choice, and 3) If already attending

church, but not spending time studying/ learning/ apply-
ing the Bible's messages, join a small group. Her inclina-
tion aside, she politely issued an invitation: "Please; I am
anxious to hear your idea."

"That's fair enough. It is at once complicated and simple. I refer to this with an acronym I call 'PHiD'. That's
right; just spit out the word! It stands for Personalized
Holographics in Discipleship. I got the *first* clue for development from a Christian archival search on Earth. That
effort revealed a printed book by Dr. R. C. Sproul entitled
"Answers to Anything Christian." The *second* clue was an
ancient television interview with a 1940s holocaust survivor from Earth's World War II.

"Let me explain: The creators of that closed circuit
project produced a hologram with a holocaust survivor in
conjunction with his pre-recorded answers to hundreds of
questions about the several years he spent in two different Nazi prison camps."

Son-tu was marginally engaged, but needed to know
more. "Exactly how did that work?"

"The producers came up with an exhaustive list of
questions anyone might ask of the survivor with regard to
his holocaust experience. The inquirer's question was automatically cued to a specific answer in his voice and with
his image! Now let's switch to my fishery project: I subsequently produced a similar program of hologram answers,
i.e., 'How to Successfully Run a Fishery-Processing
Plant.'"

He had her attention, but she hadn't yet made the
connection. She responded with, "And?"

That was apparently the invitation for which he was
waiting because he got right to the point: "I'm working on
a gospel discipleship program utilizing the same concept."

"Fish on, my friend! Are you claiming to have begun
development of a similar holographic concept for Chris-

tian discipleship? This is over the top! Allow me to pursue several obvious questions: What is the source of your questions and answers? How would distribution work? And what about funding?"

Bing-ta laughed and said, "Let's see if I can assuage your concerns with one thing at a time. First of all, I have had my after-hours Christian team working on the start-up for the past several months. We have developed some 200 or so relevant questions, but so far with only a few finished answers. What we need now are many more questions and a full slate of answers. Once that has been accomplished we will integrate everything into a micro-wave application for personal com-glass usage. Frankly, I don't understand the computer integration details, but I have access to some bright tech-savvy youngsters for that."

"Pardon a blunt follow-up to all of that, Bing-ta, but you haven't yet addressed the elephant in the room."

"Yes, that involves your second question, doesn't it? Well, I am a rare animal on Andivoli in that I am also a Christian philanthropist."

Son-tu was surprised by both statements, but skeptical as to the working of each. "Can you demonstrate this highly imaginative concept for me?"

"Uh, I think so." He looked around as if for someone in particular. "Vitaly," he said in spotting him, "our guest would like to see an example of our fishery hologram project. Will you set things up for that?"

"Bing-ta's project manager had been listening to the conversation and said, "Yes, sir, I can do that, but you know we just put the first set of questions and answers into the 'Christian Discipleship' can. Would you like to see that instead?"

"Perfect," he said, beaming.

The project manager showed Son-tu how to access the microwave app on a pair of com-glasses. Before she was asked to activate the single program's question—*What are the Attributes of God?*—Bing-ta interjected a comment: "We have to give credit for the essence of these answers from a research commentary we are calling the *Zwemke Zenith* in an appropriately named 2022 book, *Passing on the Faith to the Next Generation,* and its author, Rod Zwemke."

What instantly came up in both audio and visual hologram format was a series of different individuals with their conversational responses to the basic question. In order, they were as follows: "One of the attributes of God, my friend, is pre-existence; that God is self-caused and self-existent. In other words, nothing and no one created God. Please find this in Exodus 3:14."

A second hologram expressively said, "Another attribute of God is immutability; that is God in His nature, attributes, and will, is exempt from change. See Psalm 102:27, Malachi 3:6, and James 1:17."

A third character came up: Using his hands expressively, he said, "One of the chief attributes of God is infinity. What does that mean? God is subject to no limitations except self-limitations. See Psalm 145:3, Job 11:79, Isaiah 66:1, 1 Kings: 8:27, and Romans 11:33." The same image went on to add something to his contribution: "Another is eternity; that is, God's nature is without beginning or end. See Psalms 90:2 and 102:27, plus 1st Timothy 6:16, and Revelation 1:8."

A fourth character appeared and she said, "For me, the most important of the many attributes of God are righteousness/justness; God always does what is right and He is Himself the standard of righteousness and justness. We find supporting scriptures for this in Genesis 18:25, Deuteronomy 32:4, Psalm 19:8, Isiah 45:19, and Romans 3:25-26. Oh, and yet another attribute is sovereignty, which means that God rules perfectly and without limitation over everyone and everything in the universe. See Psalms 59:13 and 115:3, Isaiah 40; 15, Daniel 2:21, Timothy 6:15, and Revelation 19:16."

Son-tu took a deep breath, wiped a tear from each eye and said, "Bing-ta, my friend . . . efficacious, personal Christian discipleship has just taken on new meaning! If I weren't already sitting down I would take a seat!"

Bing-ta said, "Thank you for that blessing. It has been an inspired beginning. If you will pardon a near pun, I believe this little fishery operation has an enormous potential for spiritual *protein* production."

Taking her cue from his playful lead, she said, "I need to hook you up with a robotic comic I once met! Seriously, however, let me say that you are to be greatly admired for your Christian vision and the grace to back it with financial treasure."

He instantly demurred. Then, with humor, exclaimed, "The credit it not mine! The Bible tells us that people once called Herod Agrippa a god and he accepted their praise rather than giving glory to the Creator. As a result, he was immediately struck with a painful disease and died, his body was then eaten by worms."

Son-tu-the-Practical responded with, "Point taken! But if I may, how practical is the activating process of the program for the new convert?"

"Just as you saw a moment ago, all the user has to do is bring up the program and click on his or her question. The image of a human host with the answer or answers is then computer-linked with the appropriate question."

This time, Son-tu rose to a standing position, her hands clasped about her cheeks in amazement. "Your creativity and biblical application is an answer to prayer, my friend. Let's postpone our departure for Earth in order to fully engage ourselves and all our resources with you, your people, and this incredible project. As they used to say in both the sports and gambling universes, I am all in!"

Had Bing-ta perhaps known her a little better he might have danced a jig with her, right on the spot. Instead, he put his emotion into words: "That is what I have been hoping for when I first heard your broadcasts. As you say, I have been blessed with creativity and financial talent, but, you, Madam Son-tu, are the visionary for which I have prayed."

FOLLOW-THROUGH

Two hours later, and with Boxx, Wy, and Bea having joined Son-tu and Bing-ta at her request, she lost no time in saying, "Change of plans, crew! We cannot overlook such providence as has come to us through this believing and creative Andivolean." Then, with a glance and a wink towards Bing-ta, she added, "And you don't yet know the half of it."

She took a deep breath and filled them in before setting up the kicker. "Going forward, gang, here's the plan: First, we are all going to engage in working full-time with Bing-ta and his team, which may take us a month, or even two. And a big hallelujah that he will also be our philanthropist for the project."

She took yet another breath before continuing. "Hey, this is breathtaking stuff! This also means we will have to adjust our mission travel plans. Wy and Bea, I know full well that you have both been instrumental in greatly expanding Jun'or's evangelistic Rimerian Movement, which was begun by Wy's father long before my grandfather Gam'man and I arrived on Jun'or. Thankfully, for purposes of this mission we have already been blessed that you were able to place temporary leadership of that endeavor into the able hands of Johnni and Pyoter."

Bea obviously gathered that something else might be afoot and said so. "Why am I suddenly anxious as to where this is going?"

For Wy's part, he only smiled while nodding at Bea.

Boxx made the intuitive circle complete with a preemptive statement while looking intently at Son-tu, "Welcome to Mission to Mankind, Bing-ta! Oh, but wait a second, the *Boundless* can't accommodate five enthusiastic souls. Any ideas, anyone?"

Wy hadn't said anything yet, but after first glancing at Son-tu, he did. "I have on occasion been called slow, but even I grasp where this situation *must* go. I propose that we—Bea and I—camp here awhile in planting the first church on Andivoli while Son-tu and Boxx play the biblical Titus to our new Timothy."

Son-tu responded with a sigh of relief. "Well spoken,Wy! Yes, Boxx and I and Bing-ta will carry forward to Earth to put into practice what all of us will be producing at Bing-ta's fishery. We have already assigned it a new acronym; *PHiD.*" At the sound of the phonetic pronunciation she had to laugh. "Sorry, I can't help myself! The formal name is Personalized Holographics in Discipleship. We should be back in six months or so to help with things here."

Bea had a statement to make and raised her hand: "Bing-ta, to be candid, I think it is fair for you to know that were it not for the mental telepathy capabilities of we four Jun'orians, I don't know that I could go along with this assignment. But that will allow us to at least keep in touch."

That statement opened things up for Son-tu to more fully explain something, even though it was essentially for Bing-ta's benefit. "It is said that Jun'or's rebellious ancestry caused God's response in genetically bringing the telepathic 'curse' down upon its native inhabitants. If it is of any consolation to Jun'orians, when the first two humans rebelled against God by yielding to Satan's temptation, it is written that He placed the original curse of laborious work upon men and painful birthing labor upon women."

Bea raised her eyebrows and said, "May I ask a question relevant to how you have just framed Junor's telepathic curse?"

Son-tu offered a subtle nod before Bea continued.

"Can you biblically explain how such a curse can be doctrinally ascribed to God's having punished Andivoleans?

Son-tu was anticipating as much. "That is well-posited, Bea! Please allow me to elaborate. The idea of a Godly curse on Jun'or is simply humankind's supposition. You are correct in that there is no biblical substance to the theory. But according to Satan's original thinking that he might somehow be able to rise to the Creator's level, it was not only babble by him, but it led to his ejection from heaven, along with one-third of the other angels.

"Now, it is a common theory with many theologians that this curse might also have been the result of Satan's similar temptation for man to colonize and geo and bio-engineer other-planet habitation for mankind. And as for the original Andivolean colonists, their apparent curse has been low human reproduction rates.

"The Bible does say, however, that what humans or Satan generate as evil God sometimes uses for good. So, the curse of mental telepathy for the four of us with Jun'orian blood will indeed serve us with modest communication opportunities while we are away. I have learned, however, that telepathy is not always a respecter of distance. Oh, and lastly for Bing-ta's benefit—and out of full disclosure—I am not a half-breed, but a treble-breed: Jun'orian, Andivolean, and Earthling."

PRODUCTION AT THE FISHERY

To Son-tu's surprise, when all four of the original mission crew showed up at Bing-ta's fishery at the appointed early evening hour, there was a welcoming project crew of another six folks waiting for them with a table set for a quick dinner. After introductions all around and the dinner completed, Bing-ta's project coordinator, Vitaly, said, "As you can see, we have recording equipment, a set, lights, electronic Christian research resources, and anything we might need to 'raise up' this task."

With those opening remarks made, he turned to specifics. "Put on your thinking caps in writing relatively short, but concise responses for the more than 100 specific questions we have already identified to this point. Think deeply. For example, someone using the program might ask, 'Who were Jesus' twelve apostles?' Not only should they be named, but you also want to add a tip; for example, suggest the user pose follow-up questions about each individual apostle—a name at a time. You see the point!

"So, re-write what you have re-written, then have the other team sign off on your electronic entries. Once we have that completed, we will develop in the same fashion a second tranche of relevant discipleship questions and answers. The Mission Mankind crew will edit the final selections and answers for the program and the Fishery crew will then handle the hologram-adaptation work in recording and coordinating the lip-synched, appropriate images for answering the associated questions. Are there any questions?"

"Yes," one of his top fishery crew workers said as she raised her hand. "Who gets to be models for the hologram images?"

The surprised project manager glanced at Bing-ta and Son-tu for guidance, but each simultaneously extended a palm-up hand in his direction as if to say, "You're in charge!"

He took his cue and replied, "Anyone who wants to participate, check-in with Son-tu. She will see to casting assignments as well as overseeing uniform costume fitting and sewing."

Five weeks later, the finished project for the 'Christianity-Answers' version of 'PHiD' was complete. A celebration was held and the co-hosts, Son-tu and Bing-ta, recognized the project manager, assistants, and the two crews, with superlatives and a fine fish dinner. Son-tu closed the evening: "We have tested the results of your hard work and have put our collective 'go' stamp on what we hope will one day be judged a historic spiritual technologic success in terms of personal discipleship. To the Creator be the Glory!"

Bing-ta, however, would have the final word. "Again, thank you everyone, for all your unstinting efforts. Pardon the analogy, but I believe this program is going to go over like Noah's floodwater!"

PART III: ON TO EARTH

OUTWARD BOUND

The 10-day hyper jump from Andivoli to Earth brought the three crew-members into orbit around Earth. Son-tu offered a short prayer of thanks for their safe arrival and then also shared some other heavenly thoughts with the two men: "Gentlemen, the incredible sun we see is, as you know, the same sun seen from Jun'or and Andivoli because all three planets are in the same galaxy." Boxx murmured, "Preach it, *reacher*!"

She smiled, but otherwise ignored the comment and said, "Bear with me; we might all learn something: Of course each planet has very different coordinates, but only marginally greater or lesser distances *from* the sun. Nothing with that, but it brings up the obvious point about mankind's fantasy concerning the capture of energy from the sun. I did some research before we left Jun'or and it appears that Earth's scientists have achieved at least a degree of using satellite-based transformers for solar energy. Do you see that somewhat oddly-shaped satellite out the main porthole?"

The two men quickly turned to check, and a fascinated Bing-ta said, "I do. How in the world does that work? I mean given weather, changing seasons, and nighttime hours?"

"Good points," she said. "First of all, the capture is intermittent. Energy is apparently wirelessly beamed down as either microwaves or laser beams from orbiting satellites to receiving stations on Earth connected to the electrical grid."

Bing-ta persisted. "But how do they overcome the intermitting problem?"

"Ingeniously, I would say. Get this: They put a huge orbital platform such as this one in space in order to harvest sunlight where the sun essentially shines nearly 100 percent of the time. From there they send the energy to storage markets on the ground. How simple it sounds, huh?"

Boxx shook his head. "Not for me. I'm getting vertigo just from thinking about it." He then offered an impish smile in saying, "Not to belittle the subject, but which came first; the planet Earth or the planet Jun'or?"

Bing-ta replied. "Let me weigh in on that one. According to the Annals of Mankind's History, Jun'or and Andivoli were colonized by settlers from Earth, but more importantly, we can go to the Bible for the authoritative answer; specifically to Isaiah 45:18. *Not only did the Creator make the earth, but He made the earth three days before the sun, moon and the rest of the solar system.*"

Before either of the other two could respond, Bing-ta held up a hand and interjected a further qualifier. "And it is worthwhile noting that neither Jun'or nor Andivoli were fully habitable until mankind's colonizers artificially made them so."

"Ah, yes," Son-tu said with a chuckle, "that's why she is called 'Mother Earth.'"

"*Captain!*" Boxx interrupted. "Belay our tour of the heavenlies! The shipboard computer is advising us of an orbital receiving station within a fraction of one parsec."

"Be a bit more precise, navigator."

"Certainly; something like 15,000 miles."

"Great; that means that with the velocity at which we are now moving, we should be making our orbital docking within minutes."

Boxx nodded and commented, "Hopefully, it will go more smoothly than at Andivoli's orbital station."

"Guaranteed," exclaimed Son-tu. "There we were dealing with robots."

As anticipated, gaining permission from the orbital station was straight forward. The *Boundless'* gravitic-driven descent to touchdown was also smoothly accomplished. The threesome disembarked and sailed through customs before Son-tu sent a microwave text to each of the two largest Atlanta area's audio/visual microwave transmission stations.

She stated their proposition: "This is Son-tu, granddaughter of Jun'or and Earth's famed Gam'man, here on a critical mission. I am advising both your station and your major competitor of my interest in purchasing evangelistic air time. Whichever of the two makes the better offer will be given the favor of our otherwise unexpected visit from Jun'or."

Boxx was amused at her approach and said so. "Did your time and your grandfather's on Earth give you that much celebrity?"

Son-tu winked and said, "Certainly his, but let's see what a little trolling with the right kind of bait might catch."

An hour or so later brought two responses to the shipboard's computer. The first responder's offer was that of a generous air time package. There would be no charge . . . that is, provided Son-tu clearly identifies the station name and slogan every ten minutes of her messaging.

Boxx smiled, rubbed his hands together, and said, "That sounds reasonable, given the ways of Earth."

"Really?" she replied. "If the second offer is significantly better I'll simply tell that negotiator the truth; that although his call was the second, the first caller's offer was lame."

Boxx couldn't help himself from commenting. "If you don't mind my saying so, dear wife, your trolling technique seems closer to that of a gasoline-powered used car dealer's pitch than to a small church calling a new pastor whose wife plays the piano."

"So be it, cynical husband. Is prayer accompanying your critique of our mission objective in working for the LORD?"

Shortly thereafter, the second station responder's message was received: "Greetings, Son-tu. We first checked with our Andivoli partner station. Their recommendation was positive. Further, our research tells us of your historical departing presentation with Gam'man when you undertook to explain your role in the ages-old UFO mystery. Thus, our station will offer you a contract of four three-minute spots a day for one week providing you also give us exclusive rights to two interviews. As you well-know, our potential audience is much greater than any audience on Andivoli."

To that message, Boxx said to the other two, "I bow to the marketing queen of the micro airwaves."

His reference to "queen" caused Son-tu to recall a conversational moment at the time of Boxx's second visit as the security and investigative agent assigned to her upon her arrival on Jun'or with her grandfather. He surprised her by saying that although he was confused by her evangelistic broadcasting messages, he was fascinated by the messenger. He then asked her to step outside for a moment with him, away from the others.

Once outside, he had pointed to Jun'or's double moons and their joint rising nature. At the same time he uttered a poetic comment: "Do you see how the shadowy light from the two moons seems to be wistfully dancing off the side of my departmental vehicle?"

She had mischievously smiled, but did not offer encouragement of any sort.

That led him to add a further qualifier. "In fact, I would rather call it *beautiful.*"

What was speaking to her now in real time was her having unthinkingly, but telepathically read his accompanying thought, which was, "*She, too, is beautiful!*"

She also recalled that very shortly after they returned to the room they had exited, she deftly managed to pull from her small purse a mirror. With a quick look she had adjusted her hair and winked at her reflection.

The rest of the couple's story has already been told.

BROADCAST-TIME

Son-tu, Boxx, and Bing-ta met with Jarvis Jarson, manager of Atlanta's biggest micro station. Son-tu introduced herself and her partners and the manager responded with, "Call me JJ." In short order they contractually agreed to terms of the microwaved air time offer. The manager also offered a few helpful words: "We are not a Christian-themed station but I know you're going to at least talk about Jesus, salvation, and abortion. Frankly, if it weren't for your popular name-recall we wouldn't book you, but we know you'll pull listeners from all sides of the faith/no-faith spectrum."

Son-tu grimaced and said, "I won't broach anything that's not biblical, and I will stay away from human sexuality unless a caller should ask. Does that suit you?" It did.

The three got up to leave as the manager said, "Be here on time for your first three-minute broadcast at 8:00 in the morning. We would also like to do the first recorded interview with Son-tu either during mid-morning or mid-afternoon tomorrow or the next day. Let me know your preference yet today."

Once they were settled at their downtown Hyatt hotel Son-tu called for a planning session. "Okay, crew, school starts tomorrow. Have your pencils sharpened." Half-smiles ensued, but no laughs, so she added, "Lighten up, guys! Seriously, let's assess the day after the last of the recorded messages. As you know, we have a very short supply of our new mission tool *PHiD* discs for special needs, but remember that it can be downloaded from our microsite by anyone."

ON CUE

Son-tu began her first Mission to Mankind message to an audience on Earth: "It has been some time since I left Earth for Jun'or after the many years accorded me in Atlanta following what some say was a 'home run' during the seventh inning break of that historic World Series baseball game. I thank you, kind hearts. But back in real time, on our way to Earth from Andivoli a few evenings ago aboard our little spaceship *Boundless* with my husband, Boxx, and our third team member, Bing-ta, something special happened during our descent. Space was graced with light from Earth's beautiful silvery moon.

"As everyone knows, the Creator's purpose for that particular heavenly body is to provide light on the earth; to separate night from day; and to be for signs, seasons, and days, even though it only shines *part-time*.

"I am using this heavenly body introduction to remind you that the Creator's attention in seeing to the universe is *full-time*. He spoke all of creation into existence somewhere around 6,000 years ago, but that was only Part 1. What was Part II of the Creator's mission? It has been—is,

64

and will ever be—the carrier for humankind's salvation through the Messiah, Christ Jesus.

"A question is posed for us in the Holy Bible in 1st Corinthians 15:55. It reads like this: *O death, where is thy sting?* What, exactly, do those six words mean? An old church hymnal so elegantly phrases it this way: '*Death in vain forbids Him arise.*' The Holy Bible thus gives us its literal answer in verse form, which many of you know very well as John 3:16. Even *it* has two parts; the first part of which lays the verse's foundation: *For God loved the world so much that he gave his one and only Son.*

"The obvious question implied by that is 'What was the purpose for such an amazing sacrifice by the One who knew no sin? The answer lies in the second part of the verse which reads thusly: *Everyone who believes in him (Jesus the Christ) will not perish, but have eternal life.*

"Let's look at that a little more closely. In other words, when your body ceases to live, the body has obviously died . . . but your soul does not cease to exist. It continues forever. What is your soul? Your soul is who you are; your *forever* identity; your personhood.

"Okay, let me back up a bit. When you love someone dearly, you are willing to give freely to the point of self-sacrifice. Thus it was that God paid the highest price He could pay with the life of his Son. In other words, Jesus accepted the punishment due us for our rebellion against God, and *then* offered us the new life that he had bought for us.

"Now this may surprise you, but eternal life isn't only for those who believe, but for everyone. Wait! What? Yes! So the real question is this: *Where* will you spend eternal life? And as for those who do *not* believe in life after death, this means that they have simply been captured. Captured? Yes, captured! And how does one free himself or herself from capture? I will provide you with that answer and more over the rest of this week's broadcasts."

That evening, after the last of the day's three rebroadcast recordings were complete, Bing-ta said to Son-tu, "Before we get into assessment, I am curious as to how the Alphas are doing."

The 'Alphas'?"

"Of course," he laughed and explained, "the 'alphabet couple—'Y' and 'B'."

"Well, how dense am I?" she said with a smile. "Let's find out! Unfortunately, you won't get much out of this because it's strictly mental." Son-tu then focused on projecting her telepathic thoughts to the targeted twosome on Andivoli: *Greetings, Wy and Bea! I know voice inflection is not discernible via mental telepathy, but I want you to know I am excited to get somewhat caught up with you. Our days since leaving Andivoli have gone well. What updates have you relative to yourselves and your own mission kick-off?*

Both Wy and Bea had always struggled with maintaining the Jun'orian courtesy of abstention from uninvited telepathy with other Jun'orians; especially so in the case of Son-tu and Boxx, but they were glad to have this contact. Wy led their literally thoughtful response: *Things are going well for us relative to overcoming the Andivolean cultural bias accorded a pair of Jun'orians like us.*

The still-Andivolian-based pair then shared that they had developed a process whereby they learned from callers if they knew of other fellow believers meeting in anyone's homes. If so, would they give them a leader's name? That had led to a half-dozen contacts and shortly after that, acceptance of their funding offer to establish Mission to Mankind's first Andivolean church under double-M's umbrella.

After the excitement of that news had settled down, Bea turned her projected thoughts to wanting to know exactly how the Earth-assigned threesome was doing. And so with all that done, the two twosomes telepathically signed off. The three then returned to seeing to the first day's broadcast assessment to an Earth-audience. Since it was apparently too soon to have received either significant audience response or station management input, the crew settled for reviewing the essence of day two's messaging.

AWAY TEAM'S NEXT DAY

It was day two for the Mission to Mankind team. Son-tu began her broadcast message with two questions: "Folks, whether you were tuned into one of my four time-slot messages yesterday or not, this question is for everyone: What name has God given to inform us about a saved life? The answer lies within my second question, which is this: Who do **you** think Jesus is?

"The answer to both questions is the same. There is salvation *in no One else*! God has given no other name under heaven by which we must be saved (Acts 4:12). No other religious teacher has, or could, die for our sins; no other religious teacher has, or could, come to Earth as God's only Son; and no other religious teacher has, or could, rise from the dead."

Son-tu turned to glance at Boxx, who nodded and held up two fingers. By that he was meaning to remind her about delivering the day's anti-infanticide exhortation. She returned his nod without missing a beat and said, "And speaking of sin, let me note by example that Earth's United States of America has off and on legalized abortion.

"The word 'abortion' is a dismissive term for infanticide, the killing of a baby in its first year of life. Incredibly, that reality—if not the legality—lives among you today. I offer this question for your consideration: 'How can any individual or society—claiming to be part of humanity—defend and practice such inhumane behavior as murdering an unborn infant? If you have questions or comments, please register them with this station and I will consider addressing one or two on-air.

INTERVIEW

The station manager (SM) began the first Mission to Mankind interview with a short intro. "I want to thank our online audience for tuning into the first of several interviews with our special guest from Jun'or and former celebrated resident of Earth, Son-tu." With that, he nodded to her and asked his first question:

SM: "What is the purpose of this return visit to Earth?"

SON-TU: "Thank you. I thought you would never ask." She waited a beat for the likely online laugh. "Quite simply," she continued, a bit more relaxed, "the mission of my crew and I is quite simple; to share the gospel with humankind, wherever found."

SM: "Is it exclusively the Christian gospel of salvation that you share?"

SON-TU: No, there are two other critical biblical elements about which we are called to evangelize."

SM: "What is the first?"

SON-TU: "Let me give you an illustration by a like-minded thinker who has the highest of scientific and DNA investigative qualifications and who has written—in what has been called the Jeanson Correlation—about the theory of evolution. He offers a metaphor: 'What would it take for a building to build itself? First, all direct human participants would have to be removed from the construction site. No construction workers, no foremen, no engineers could be present. Instead, some sort of unfathomable, random self-assembly would commence.'"

SM: "That's graphic!"

SON-TU: "Yes, but the metaphor not only relates to our evolutionary computer chip's *spontaneously* producing a building, but then also spitting out a *second* computer chip; likewise continuing by itself with the process of construction and reproduction."

SM: "I see the point. There is no plan for design, yet there is the expectation of such. If we may, let's move on with your broader agenda. What is the remaining critical subject of your mission?"

SON-TU: "Again, thank you. Another Christian writer, no less qualified in his field than the former, addresses the subject of maternal infanticide. Again, infanticide is murder of a child in the first year of life by its mother. Those who would hear me, please understand that this is a subject I find as compelling and repulsive as does the author of the aforementioned tome. Why? As R. B. Kuter writes, 'There is no person who should receive the authority to take the life of another human being simply because they *choose* to do so.' I will be sharing more from what I call the 'Kuter Critique' during this week's succeeding messages."

SM: "Thank you, Son-tu. We appreciate your time. We will be interviewing you a second time on another day."

BOXX'S BIBLE STUDY

Two days later, Boxx excitedly shared something special with Son-tu. "As I was screening a caller yesterday—a young adult male—who said that he had been listening to your messages and the earlier interview, and wanted to know if we would be hosting a Bible study. It took me a full three seconds before I answered with, 'Yes, we could. Are you part of a Christian-believing church?'

"He responded in the positive and added that his was only a small, local home church, and since they only have half a dozen regulars and no trained pastor, they are forced to rotate the teaching among the group's lay members.

"What could I say except that I would temporarily make myself available. I asked for his name and address and actually set up my first meeting with his group for tomorrow evening. If the other members are as enthusiastic as this fellow and are willing to meet for an hour or so twice a week for as long as we are in the area, I am good. We can also try to attract others with like interests. Why don't you mention this during your segments and interviews? I think I'll call the course *At Long Last, Born Again.*"

"Wow! Great name! From where did you get that?"

"From what I've been reading of the personal lessons of Harry Ironside, a late 19th and early 20th century American Bible teacher and pastor, once known as 'the Boy Preacher.' His story is intriguing. A traveling evangelist pressed upon a young Ironside that God would stop his mouth until the boy actually had sight of Christ (Romans 3:19). That's deep! In other words, the boy only *presumed* he was saved."

Son-tu was impressed and immensely proud of her husband. "Boxx," she said, "that is terrific! I will definitely plug the course for you. I can't wait to share with Wy and Bea your obviously heart-felt call for Bible study leadership."

"Good! I told him I would also introduce a special discipleship mentoring tool for their use. He was game for everything, adding that he has a large house for meeting purposes."

SECOND INTERVIEW

The station manager began Son-tu's second interview the final day of the week's evangelical messaging schedule.

SM: "During your first interview concerning Earth and creationism you teased and intrigued us with something you called the 'Jeanson Correlation' and its having to do with the Y Chromosome tree and the Holy Bible's claim about all peoples having descended from Shem, Ham, and Japheth."

Considering that it was unusual for a neutral interviewer to be enthusiastic about any interviewee's subject, he nevertheless continued: "You said that 'unfolding' deals with the beginning of human history and a small group of people who began making bricks. Bricks! You even shared how they baked them and married the bricks with mortar concocted from a tarlike substance combined with sand and gravel." He hesitated a moment before saying, "I'm sorry. I think I'm stealing your thunder. Please expand along those lines."

SON-TU: "That's okay," she said with a laugh. "The people's purpose was to build for themselves a city and a tower reaching unto the heavens, but it had nothing to do with worshipping the Creator. In fact, the concept was totally at odds with the Creator's commands. So, out of that, the Creator God judged the people and scattered them, while also supernaturally inhibiting their ability to work together. The result of God's judgment thus rendered the people foolish in both their talk and actions. That, then, is the source of our modern-day word 'babble.'"

SM: "So the people of Babel—I presume somewhere in the Middle East—moved away, but to where?"

SON-TU: "The Jeanson Correlation surmises that with detailed research into Y chromosome mutation rates, they went to extra-continental locations like China, New Guinea, Australia, and the Americas. Realize now that the dispersed families would have restarted their lives with only a portion of the technological knowledge they once had as a larger community at Babel. In other words, their immediate way of life would have been simple—or to use Jeanson's word—'primitive'."

SM: "So, how does all of this connect with the mainstream version of human history—you know—the Neanderthals, the Stone Age, and the Agricultural Revolution?"

SON-TU: "Those times would have transpired within the early centuries. Jeanson assesses it this way: 'Humanity continued to progress from 'primitive' to 'advanced', but that transition was rapid, consistent with the needs and trials of recently dispersed bands of people arriving in previously uninhabited areas.'"

SM: "That is fascinating. I have to say that this station has received hundreds of calls these past few days in response to your messaging, Son-tu. You have also said that many have indicated interest in your core message. Is there anything else you would like to add to our interview?"

SON-TU: "Yes. First, I am troubled about the age-old challenge of discipleship for new believers. You see, salvation is merely the first step in a believer's life. Aside from those who are truly motivated to seek out a church for Christian growth, how does an individual grow spiritually from the point of salvation unless he or she has either a support group or some kind of tutorial program?

SM: "Now that is a very interesting point. Is there a practical answer?

SON-TU: "That is perhaps the most exciting aspect of this mission. The measure of any church or evangelical organization is not its size, but the depth of its ability to disciple the newly saved. To that end, we have developed a one-of-a-kind discipleship tutorial utilizing holograms. It is available free of charge on auto-comline. We are also introducing it in person at a newly formed home church gathering this very evening for anyone who would like to visit. This station will provide particulars for those interested in attending."

FURTHER INTO THE FRAY

Over the balance of the first week's broadcasts and all but the final day of the second week, Son-tu continued with her pointed three-pronged evangelizing for creationism and salvation, plus excoriation of infanticide. This would be the final day of the first phase of the broader mission on Earth. As for the surprising home church opportunity, it went beautifully with nearly fifty people in attendance. In addition, the original caller subsequently made a decision to take on leadership, with initial in-person support from Boxx.

Son-tu began the closing day's broadcast with appreciation for her continually growing audience. "Before I conclude this phase of our mission on Earth, I want to thank you, our listeners and viewers, for your indulgence and the many who have been moved to positively respond to our messages. I especially congratulate those who have been called to actively participate in several small local groups with my husband Boxx. For the initial gatherings, these groups will continue to be in-person at the host homes but then, the studies will be conducted through a combination of local in-person leadership and online electromagnetic microwave media."

She briefly paused to focus on a new thought but then blinked in apparently settling her mind about something. "Folks, what I am about to say will not only surprise *you,* but also the rest of our crew!" Boxx snapped his head in her direction and then towards Bing-ta as if to say, *Uh, oh, now what?*

"Master Boxx and I, along with our newest missionary, Master Bing-ta, will shortly be departing for. . . Ukraine . . . with the message of the gospel!" Having uttered that shocker she turned to capture Boxx's expression, which was one of winced surprise.

There were a few moments of verbal white space before she reconnected with her audience. "Sorry for the surprise digression, folks, but please allow me to leave you with some critical closing comments about genetic findings matching biblical predictions. This I have taken directly from the Jeanson Correlation.

"Long before we knew about the genetics of pre-DNA technology, Darwin proposed that all creatures developed from a common ancestor via small changes over a long time. But new findings in the field of genetics tell a far different story. The Bible's time frame of roughly some 6,000 years correctly predicts the total number of genetic mutations which have been discovered in the tiny string of DNA in certain aspects of human cells.

"So what?" you are probably thinking. Well, if humans have been around for some 6,000 years, the number of these mutations should be about 80. If they have been around 200,000 years or more, as evolutionists claim, the number should be half a dozen times more than that number. The actual number, however, is right around 80! So now you see why the term *correlation* is used relative to creationism.

"Okay, I know I am boring half of my audience and the other half has already turned me off, but a thinking person should ask *this* question: 'Is this just what we would expect if all humans came from three women who got off Noah's Ark just a few thousand years ago?' Acts 17:29a leads us to the answer: *From one man God created all the nations.* Conclusion: There is only one race: *Homo sapiens*! Please support the efforts of Mission to Mankind, and thank you for tuning in. This has indeed been a genuine privilege."

POST-BROADCAST

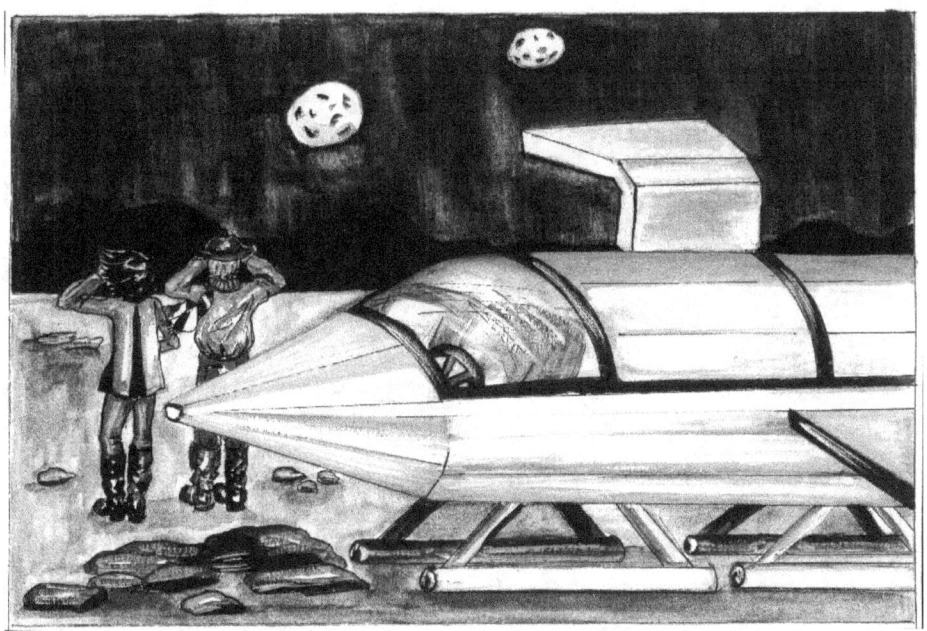

Illustration drawn by Boxx many years ago of he and Son-tu observing Jun'or's two moons from a nearby planetary observatory.

"Ukraine?!" Boxx exclaimed, close to either fuming or exulting; it was hard to tell which. "So, dear wife," he continued, "Bing-ta and I found this out at the same time as our audience?"

"Sorry," Son-tu said, raising her shoulders and sighing, "but I have been thinking about this for some time. This is the thirtieth year since the 2022 Putin/Russia carnage of Ukraine. That eastern European country has since made a remarkable come-back from that long-ago episode and Russia's long disdain for Ukrainian nationhood. I recall that at the time, one of Vladimir Putin's puppet cabinet members wrote this: 'After the Russian victory, the Ukrainian state will disappear, just like the Nazi Third Reich.'

"Of interest to us is that Ukraine not only remains the 'breadbasket of Europe,' but is also a fertile area for the Christian harvest. There is no reason not to think there are as many people there as before who fear man more than God. This calling has been made clear for me this very morning. As for its details, God seems to be leaving that for us to sort out."

The third voice in the room—Bing-ta's—was then heard, and not without a wry sense of humor. "I have obviously been drafted into this next phase, but I am not certain as to whether I am being blessed with fate or with a brick!"

The twosome laughed and Son-tu proceeded with some rebuttal. "Don't misunderstand what I am about to say, but this decision causes me to think of an analogy to what the biblical Paul said to some of those he had been teaching: 'It is time to stop drinking milk and begin eating solid food!' With that, she turned to Boxx to say, "Husband, partner, and tour leader, would you see to the details of this surprise, upcoming Kiev tour, including arrangements for a musical worship group?"

Boxx had no problem with immediately taking ownership of his expanded role. "My suggestion is to try contacting the son of Vadim Kaletsey of the New Jerusalem Band, formerly headquartered in Minsk, Belarus. You may remember my having mentioned that while on Earth the senior Kaletsey and his band performed at Gam'man's invitation to speak at the World Series event, which preceded my Andivolean coming-out speech."

A few hours later, following dinner, with the two of them alone, Son-tu said, "You know, honey, I really appreciate your creative thinking, not to mention being the adjutant-glue holding everything and every one of us together."

She apparently caught Boxx by surprise because he put down some papers, took her hand and pulled her to him, saying, "I love you, wife. You are not only the leader of this mission, but also the true encourager, just as you have been since we first met."

"Thank you, Boxx, but we all have a role to play in our lives with one another. I will never forget the second time we met involving Jun'or's twin moons."

Boxx smiled. "Yes, that was a bit more intimate. I was fortunate to have been able to arrange for you to come with me on a vendor's gig to a mountain observatory."

"Boy, do I remember that," she said, nodding. "It was incredible! Before returning home, the vendor pilot took us up another one-thousand feet or so in his gravity-driven transit craft and we viewed the binary moons with hand-held telescopes. One of the moons housed the prison at which my grandfather was once held. The pilot took a photo framing us while glassing the moons, but I never saw it."

"Yes, I know. I didn't like the photo and threw it away. But when we got back I drew an illustration from memory." With that, he reached into a pocket as he said, "I have kept a copy of it in my wallet ever since." He handed it to her, saying, "See what you think."

She took the picture, looked at it longingly and said through glistening eyes, "This is wonderful. Why have you never shown it to me before?"

"Because I didn't think it was very good."

FIRST SERVICE IN UKRAINE

Bomb destruction of a home in Ukraine by invading Russian government in 2022.

Back at their quarters, the three of them sat down to discuss things. Boxx began with a question, "Son-tu, how long do you think it will take to properly arrange this suddenly announced pilgrimage?"

"Well, some of Earth's international evangelistic organizations would say a year, but knowing your talents, you can probably manage in not much more than a month. The first thing I will do to get you a leg-up is call around the Atlanta area for the name of a strong local church and a missions leader with Ukrainian church-planting contacts." Without waiting for comment on that by her two cohorts, she continued.

"Boxx, why don't you first arrange for our passports? Then you can begin securing appropriate supplies. Bing-ta, I know this is short notice, but can you arrange for your own personal needs as well as being prepared to help either of us according to mission particulars?"

Bing-ta's expression mirrored that of a traffic light having just turned green. As for his verbal reaction, he used only three words: "Here am I."

By the end of the day Son-tu had the name of the missions' pastor of a recommended metro Atlanta area church who for years had been intimately involved in planting a number of churches around the world, including Ukraine. She reached him by com-glass the next morning and he was delighted to hear of her broad plans. He not only provided her with the name of at least one church and pastor in that area, but they also talked at some length. Of particular interest to her was one unexpected aspect.

He said, "I am in the process of planning a trip to Ukraine in undertaking a formal installation at the newest of our church's plants. Would your crew be interested in joining forces with me for that visit?"

Barely six weeks later the four of them boarded *Boundless* and made short work of traveling to Kyiv, Ukraine. Quickly passing through customs, they boarded a ten-year old electric van to make their way to the mission pastor's church plant some thirty miles away. There was still evidence of the brutal and almost total destruction once having been thrust onto the area by Russia and its madman czar, Vladimir Putin. The foursome assessed that the countryside's wheat fields were not only ready for the agricultural harvest, but that there must also be countless Ukrainian souls ripe for the message of the things of eternity.

As they entered the small church—recently built with their guide's American church planting funds—the U.S. pastor and guide said, "Whenever I enter a church we have planted I immediately feel as if I'm home. This visit, however, is going to be very special because this is the 200th Redeemer church we have planted since our founding in 1996."

The guide introduced the three visitors and the host pastor to each other, commenting, "This is the first time I've been to Ukraine without needing a local interpreter." He then explained to the local pastor that Son-tu was fluent in many languages, including both Ukrainian and Russian.

The service and ceremony took place the following day. That was Sunday, of course, and the service began with the host pastor opening with thanksgiving and prayer before the American guide carried out the moving installation ceremony and introduction of the other three visitors. All of that was with the help of Son-tu's interpretive skill. The host pastor then surprised the congregation by saying, "Our guest speaker today is well known on all three worlds. Please make Evangelist Son-tu welcome."

The assembled congregation of about fifty men and women, along with a few young children, were delighted to hear the speaker address them in their own language. She thanked them and put the congregation further at ease by saying, "I neither think of myself as preacher or teacher, but *reacher!*" That was greeted by both laughter and applause.

She then offered a few more words of appreciation for the pastor's invitation to speak, and their guide's strong church support. This was followed by a humorous comment about having traveled to their church by two similar modes of transportation: "The first leg was via a gravity-driven spaceship from planet Jun'or to Earth and then to Kyiv. The second leg was in a rented Ukrainian van from Kyiv to your church." That drew even broader laughter.

Holding up a Ukrainian language Bible she said her subject would be on the Beatitudes from the Gospel of Matthew. She reminded everyone that it was Jesus, the Christ, who gave us the pronouncements of the Eight Beatitudes in the Sermon on the Mount near the Sea of Galilee, and that it was recorded for all posterity in the first book of the New Testament. "Jesus," she said, "offers us a way of life that promises eternity in the Kingdom of Heaven."

She went on to explain that the message of Jesus is one of humility, charity, and brotherly love, and that they promise us eternal salvation—not in this world, but in the next. "What is a biblical Beatitude?" she asked rhetorically. "One definition is this: a possession of all things held to be good, from which nothing is absent that a good desire may want." She thought about something for another beat or two, and then added, "Perhaps a clearer meaning of a Beatitude would be comparing it with its opposite; misery!

"Each of the Beatitudes tells how to be blessed by God. So what does' blessed' mean?" Someone shouted "Happiness!" in Ukrainian.

"Yes," she said. "But it means more than mere happiness. It implies the fortunate or enviable state of those who are in God's Kingdom." She stopped for a moment, wanting to focus her next comments on these people's daily lives. "Having lived in beautiful Ukraine all your lives I'll bet you still know what it means to be miserable at some time or another. So, yes, misery sometimes means being afflicted unwillingly with painful sufferings. So, as we see in such a case as that, happiness is a choice."

She ended her message with another reminder of the war in Ukraine which had taken place only thirty years earlier: "Tens of millions around this planet prayed for people in this very community." Following that was a solemn altar call at which more than a dozen people came forward in accepting Christ as their LORD and Master.

As the four were preparing to leave the church, a young couple with grim countenances approached Son-tu. Speaking in Ukrainian, the woman said, "I want to tell you of something I once witnessed."

She began her story: "First of all, thank you for remembering Russia's latest war against us. I was twenty-nine years old in 2022. Russian government soldiers had just gathered a group of children in our village. They struck each one of them and then told them to run away. When the children had reached a certain distance between them and the soldiers, the soldiers—incredibly—aimed their rifles and used the children for target practice. Some were shot in the legs, others in the back, and others . . ." She couldn't finish her sentence. After a moment the woman pushed her hair behind her ear and pulled her husband to her as she finished her comments. "I do not know if any survived, but our own child did not."

Son-tu took her hand in both sympathy and empathy. "Thank you for sharing such a tragic event with us. I cannot imagine such a life's impact on any parent."

But it wasn't only that couple who approached. An older man also came up to share. Tightly holding the brim of his hat with both hands below his waist he tearfully spoke in good English: "My name is Ivan. During the Russian government invasion thirty years ago I served at the underground Emergency Field Hospital in Lviv in Western Ukraine. Just before that I helped out as a volunteer with RII (Reach Initiative International), a humanitarian organization providing compassionate help to Jewish holocaust survivors and Ukrainian refugees in Israel."With that introduction, he began what he wanted to share: "One of the saddest days of my life occurred when outgoing food container ships were being blocked in the Black Sea by the Russian government." His eyes betrayed what he was about to say.

"In order to stretch resources for dependent recipients, we had already cut meager rations in half, but then . . . in order to help the many, we were forced to cut them even further. Do you know what that action meant?"

Son-tu took his hand and said, "I have no idea, my friend."

Tearfully, he replied, "We had to take food from the hungry in order to feed the starving. I just wanted to say thank you for bringing the message of Jesus saves to Ukrainians."

POST SERVICE

WHEN THE SPIRIT OF GOD FELL ON AN ENTIRE PEOPLE

During Billy's 1973 five-day crusade in Seoul, South Korea, more than 3.2 million people attended the meetings. During the closing service there were more than 1.1 million people present, the largest live audience ever for an evangelistic message. The amazing photo above was taken that same closing day at a paved runway a mile long and 200 yards wide. –Decision Magazine

As the four silently made their way back to their van for the return trip to Kyiv, Boxx was forthcoming about the service. "I thought everything went very well."

The threesome's American pastor was more enthusiastic. "I have witnessed many new church installations around the world and can say I have never seen one as moving as the one tonight."

Son-tu nodded in agreement. "From my perspective, we also just witnessed confirmation that our decision to come to Ukraine has been guided by the LORD. Now, however, we need to focus on our plans for the upcoming five-day evangelistic crusade in Kyiv. Who has thoughts on the subject?"

Boxx was anxious to respond. "With the amazing help of our well-connected American pastor/guide here and the many organizational tour tips graciously shared by the BGEA in the state of North Carolina, we are well under way with orchestrating things for this beautiful spring, outdoor event. Some from that evangelistic organization have even gone so far as to say what we are planning may rival some of their own crusades."

Bing-ta weighed in with several comments. "That my friend, is indeed a compliment, but we will not be approaching anything like the 80-year-ago crusade held in 1973 in Seoul, South Korea by the legendary Billy Graham. In the course of the upcoming five days of our meetings, I'm hoping we pull close to 50,000 folks from Ukraine and its surrounding former Soviet Union countries, and perhaps even some from far-Western Russia."

"Speaking of that truly incredible, long-ago Billy Graham event," Boxx interjected as he pulled up some notes, "with the blessing of many area churches, we've made headway in arranging for discounted hotel fees and charter bus and railroad service for folks coming from the four winds, but I don't think we'll see a fraction of that kind of turn-out, much less the thousands camping on hillsides as in the days of Jesus's ministry in Galilee."

Son-tu further added to the appreciative note. "When we return to Jun'or we need to be certain about returning a meaningful thank-you to each and every contributing church and organization."

Boxx nodded in agreement. "I will personally see to that, but you, dear wife, get credit for being leader of the leaders!"

Son-tu sensed that Boxx seemed about to add something else to his comment so she waited. Sure enough, he was. "Oh, and by the way, I just received a response from Vadim, Jr. concerning your musical request."

She was all ears, but said nothing for fear of being disappointed.

"Well, let's see now," he teased, "when I mentioned your name and our upcoming tour in Kyiv, he . . . *jumped* on it! You, of course, would not know he long ago immigrated to Ukraine. And get this: He said he would even write for our event a special arrangement of *Island Moon*; one of your favorites."

She released some tears in the process of clapping her hands to her face. "Yes! Thank you, thank you, thank you!" she exclaimed. "That is such a beautiful ballad written during Earth's so-called Second World War by an old friend of my grandfather."

Bing-ta had not joined in with much of the mutual admiration society, so Son-tu felt led to reiterate an earlier conversation with him. "You know, gentlemen, our Andivolean native here, has again declined accepting personal compliments concerning the *PHiD* project." With a wink at him she said, "Let me assure him that everything is good with us. I have *de-wormed* all four of us by thanking the LORD in advance, during, and at the end of each of these first Ukrainian days together." Everyone had a hearty laugh, the loudest being Bing-ta's.

TO KYIV

Satan being cast down from Heaven (Revelation 12).

The Jun'orian crew dropped their American Baptist church guide off at the Kyiv airport for his trip back home via commercial aircraft, and thanked him profusely for his invaluable help. They then kept their appointment at a downtown hotel with Viktor, their local mission coordinator. Viktor welcomed them and shook hands with each of the three. He straightened his tie and appeared to be nervous. With excellent English, however, he said, "I and my team are excited to be a part of this historic Christian crusade, but we still have much work to do."

"Thank you," Son-tu said. "We appreciate all you and your volunteers have done, but first, tell us what we should know about Ukraine."

"Seriously?" he said, obviously impressed to be asked that question.

"Of course," she replied in returning his suddenly brightened smile.

"Thank you for that. If you will pardon my lecture style, allow me to give you a short crash course. Before I became a capitalist businessman I taught eastern European history at the university. Going back a little further, in June of 1941 Hitler attacked the Soviet Union. My grandparents lived here in Kyiv at the time. After 77 years of a peaceful life, they once again found themselves counting the slices of bread they had left, and keeping water jars in every room in the naïve hope of extinguishing fire from an enemy rocket.

"The czarist empire of the 20th century considered Ukrainians no more than a regional branch of the Russian people. In 1920, we became a Ukrainian Soviet Republic, the true foundation of modern Ukrainian statehood. To this very day Russia still celebrates Stalin while Ukraine has undergone a profound democratic revolution. Thirty years ago, as you know, an ethnic avenger of Stalin's genocidal famine of Ukrainians was in power in the form of a Ukrainian Jewish President. Over time he would come to secure a place alongside other wartime leaders under imminent threat such as Judah Maccabee, Abraham Lincoln, and Winston Churchill."

Now it was Son-tu who was impressed. "I seem to recall that Putin tried blaming his country's invasion as liberating Russian-sympathizers from a neo-Nazi government."

Viktor laughed a tone of incredulity. "Ukraine's President, Velodymyr Zelenskyy, was Jewish! I don't believe he was a Messianic Jew, as I am, but as a follower of Jesus I know that if Jesus had not been Jewish, He could not have fulfilled God's covenant promise that the seed of Abraham would bless the world."

Son-tu had been about to thank the professor for his excellent input, but his last comments compelled her to pursue things a bit further. "Viktor, you just opened another page of my mind and heart. I am a student of the book of Genesis and I wonder what you have to say about Adam and Eve's son Cain having murdered his righteous brother Abel. Do you think that was an attempt by Satan to destroy the Messianic line?"

That question caught the professor by surprise. He smiled broadly and said, "Yes, my dear, you are indeed a student of the Word. But Eve birthed Seth, who continued the line. Satan's goal is to rule the world instead of God, and have all humanity worship him (Isa. 14:12-14).

"Consequently, he has tried to destroy the woman and her Seed since he first heard God's promise of a Redeemer in Genesis 3:15. Your point represents the first of Satan's more than a dozen attempts with his plan, not only before Jesus's birth but again before His crucifixion. And he will continue to do so until the Christ's second coming. And that is what is referred to in Revelation 12 as War in Heaven. The Holy Spirit cannot fail because He is God."

With that, Viktor grimaced and said, "I'm sorry. I didn't mean to run off the rail, but since the fall of humanity the world has been trying to exchange the truth of God for a lie."

"No apology needed. On the contrary, you are obviously being used of God to advance the Kingdom. Now, if you would, please bring us up to speed relative to how things look for our crusade one week hence."

The middle-aged Ukrainian Bible teacher and mission coordinator then shared with Son-tu and the others about the promotional print and electronic streaming ads to run in the capital cities of its seven bordering countries, plus the three largest cities in Ukraine—Kyiv, Kharkiv, and Odessa. He continued with various details of their preparation and added, "We have also advertised that Son-tu's interview messages will be delivered in the Ukrainian language."

DAY ONE OF THE FIVE-DAY KYIV CRUSADE

The first afternoon's message opened amid brilliant sunshine, but not too hot on this early spring day. In addition to the rolling hillside's grass-padded field, air time had been purchased through the largest band microwave stations in Kyiv, some both audio and video, but a few audio only. A few of the outlets were secular, meaning that messaging which fell outside of their guidelines was priced at double the standard rate. In other words, censorship for those stations was more a matter of price than principle, but for the online streaming com-glass users, it was a global option.

Strangely, although Son-tu would not be aware of it until later in the day, some recipients outside Ukraine who did not know either Ukrainian or Russian said they somehow understood the message in their own language. That was baffling to everyone except those who know that God sometimes works His way through man's effort to spread the Good News. In any event, no matter a person's nationality or language, the Holy Spirit speaks to all who want to hear (Acts 2:6-8).

Viktor had seen to it that multiple loud speaker amplifiers were placed throughout the huge and recently mown grassy hillside fields, which backed gently away from the elevated grandstand. Some estimates still projected as many as 50,000 people would be gathered. Son-tu pondered the miracle of Christ having addressed such crowds, His voice reaching everyone without electronic amplification. But then, neither will the world fail to hear Jesus' triumphant trumpet call at His return!

"Greetings to all!" she began. "My name is Son-tu. By virtue of life experience on Earth and its colonized planets, Jun'or and Andivoli, I am a citizen of all three, but do we not all owe life itself to the Creator? Allow me to pose a question for you. Do you know with certainty what happens when you close your eyes for the last time? This is a crucial question, but there is also a second question directly related to the first. Do you know that the Creator God has implanted a desire in each of us to live . . . *forever*? Now, how do we know that?

"History absolutely confirms that Jesus the Christ, who lived in the Middle East some 2,000 years ago, died and returned from the dead. Now, if Jesus died and returned from the dead, then He is not only an eyewitness to the afterlife, but He is the Son of God who *created* this afterlife.

"What is the first thing we can take from that? It is this: We will all exist *somewhere* for eternity! In other words, as the Holy Bible's disciple John puts it, '*Everyone who believes in Him (Jesus the Christ) will not perish, but will have eternal life.*'

"Again, the second point about this verse is equally important: *Where* will we spend eternal life? Through the sinless Jesus's sacrificial life the door has been flung open for anyone who comes to Him in repentance and faith. Yes, that we might gain immortality through His taking us with Him to heaven! Thus, do you see why we are inborn to a longing for life after death?

"And what a life it will be! Yet you may also ask how we can be certain of *this*. The God who brought the vast galaxies into existence and designed the intricacies of a life-giving atmosphere with humans, animals and plants, not to mention magnificent mountains and enormous seas, is obviously creative and powerful enough to provide an eternal and joyful experience for heart-felt believers.

"There is another way of putting what I just said. It comes from the Holy Bible in 1st Corinthians 2:9, which reads, '*What no eye has seen, what no ear has heard, and what no human mind has conceived—the things God has prepared for those who love him.*'

"Let me close today's message by admitting that anyone could *claim* to be God! The Jesus who claimed to be divine, however, died of His own volition and then rose from the dead on the third day . . . well, that is pretty good evidence that He is telling the truth. *Now*, I am speaking *directly* to all those within earshot of my voice, that in spite of our human limitations and failures, the LORD is sovereignly directing His own work of redemption through human evangelism. Yes, ladies, gentlemen, and children, this applies through the evangelism which has this very day been brought to Ukraine and its surroundings!"

ASSESSMENT OF MESSAGING

The full team gathered after the attendance masses had scattered to find the many authorized food purveyors which had been positioned for the day's mid-afternoon break following the opening two-hours of the crusade. An adequate number of portable *relief* structures had also been seen to for people's needs. The second teaching segment would begin in another hour.

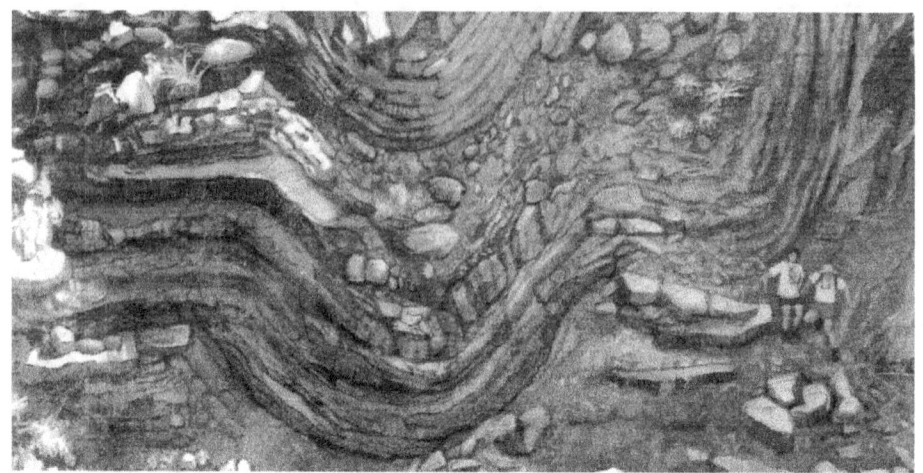

ARE THESE ROCK LAYERS MILLIONS OF YEARS OLD?
This real-life photo illustrates that while there are many examples of catastrophism that support the creation-based biblical worldview, one of the most significant is the presence of warped rocks in Earth's Grand Canyon. This visual evidence shows multiple layers that once bent and flowed together without breaking.

Boxx was anxious to update Son-tu with routine input telepathically provided by the Andivoli gatekeepers-extraordinaire—Wy and Bea Chesser. Surprisingly, she said, "Not now, Boxx. Everyone needs to continue doing what has to be done. I have to focus on what is directly before me. We have four and a half days to go."

She began the next session with the biblical passage most believers call the single most dramatic conversion in history. "Please settle down so that you can focus on what I am about to share. It involves the most miraculous con-version event of the Bible. It took place with Saul, a Greek-speaking Jew who was traveling north from Jeru-salem some 2,000 years ago. He had nearly reached Da-mascus in Syria, intent on rooting out followers of The Way—that is, followers of Jesus. "He was suddenly knocked to the ground and blinded by a blaze of light.

Then he heard a voice say, "Saul, Saul, why do you persecute me?"

"Who are you, Lord?" asked the stricken Saul.

"'I am Jesus, whom you are persecuting,' said the voice, 'but rise and enter the city, and you will be told what you are to do.'"

Son-tu was speaking with the sort of heightened commentary we might have expected of one of Saul's own traveling companions. "Saul let the men traveling with him lead him by the hand to Damascus. Once there, he spent three days in a kind of stupor. Then a follower of The Way by the name of Ananias restored his sight, and 'something like scales fell from his eyes.' Saul, the persecutor, was not only baptized but immediately began a new life as the man who would be known to history as the Apostle Paul.

"Now, you folks hearing this, rest assured that you will not be struck blind and left in a stupor today, but by the will of God, before today's session ends you will have the opportunity to become a saved follower of Christ Jesus.

"But first, I have another, very different question for you!" Son-tu took a deep breath and asked the key question of the crusade. "Why is the single most critical event in all of history related to Jesus, the Messiah? Etch this into your heart because the answer to this question is for every single person within my hearing! *For God made Christ, who never sinned, to be the offering for our sin, so that we could be made right with God through Christ* (2nd Cor. 5:21).

"So I ask, do you simply know *of* Jesus, or do you actually *know* Jesus? What's the difference? Knowing Christ is having a personal relationship with Him. Think for a moment about any person who might quickly come to mind. Do you simply *know* him or her—that is, are you simply acquainted with him or her—or do you have a *personal relationship* with that person? Do you see the difference, folks?"

She took in another deep breath before making a surprising, if welcome statement. "Why don't each of you—those who are able—stand for a moment and stretch your arms and legs before sitting back down. I'm sorry we don't have two fish and five loaves of bread with which to ask God to feed you, but as you can see, there is opportunity around you when we have finished our business together." She waited for the delayed laughter that would come.

"This is my final question of this segment and it is not rhetorical! How many of you firmly believe that if Jesus were here in person at this very moment He could not only feed every one here with only a few fish and loaves of bread at His disposal?" She cupped her hands around both ears and repeated herself, this time shouting. "Let me hear you!" She was rewarded with a tremendous cheer.

"Hallelujah! Okay, now that you have stretched your bodies, I want you to exercise your minds. Consider how it is that each and every one of us first came to be. That's right, how God not only fundamentally allows for life to be created and for the perpetuation of the human race, but also everything we can see and about which we can learn. Look around you at everything your eyes, ears, and mind can take in. Is anything more foundational than creation itself? Absolutely not!

"There is an explanation for all of this. Not only does there have to be a Creator, but I know Him personally. Yes, and I trust His account of past events. After all, He was there, folks. That's because He was *doing* it all. In the words of one of my many fine theological collaborators over the years and decades, 'the climactic, crowning act of God in creation was the creation of the human race. Created *last* in terms of time, human beings were *first* in importance.'

"Now I know what some of you are thinking: What about evolution?' Consider this: If people are simply the product of millions of years of evolution beginning with some unknown gasses or primeval slime and mud; then humanity is not to be significantly distinguished from the animal world from which it supposedly sprang; and life loses purpose and worth.

"People sometimes ask *why* they were created. The Creator Himself *answers* that question: You and I were created to proclaim with our mouths and demonstrate with our lives the intrinsic, eternal perfections of God . . . and to enjoy Him forever!

"Yes, we were created for God's benefit. So how are we doing? I know; not very well! But that doesn't change *why* we were created. We still have a job to do. So let's look at that for a moment and then I'll be through.

"Scientifically speaking, at the dawn of human history, humanity was in an advanced state. The people spoke a single language and together they set about to build a city and a tall tower called Babel (Genesis 11). In defiance of God, they wanted to reach the heavens. That is called humanism in that it *elevates* people and *denigrates* God.

"Those people, like millions of people today—were and are—living as though this were the only life that counted. They completely lost sight of eternity. At the time we are illustrating, divine judgment was handed down for their disobedience. What happened? God scattered people all over the earth, and these migratory bands not only began to speak regionally different languages but they also entered a short period of cultural primitiveness. It was from this that they eventually emerged to *pro*gress rather than *re*gress.

"Hear me, folks: Time never performs miracles! The fossil record shows no evidence that any basic category of animal has ever evolved from or into any other basic category. The more time there is, the more extinction, and the greater number of harmful mutations will occur. So what we *then* have is *de*-volution instead of *e*-volution. In yet other words, time is the *enemy* of evolution, rather than its hero.

"One of the most significant examples of catastrophism that support the creation-based biblical worldview is the presence of warped rocks in Earth's Grand Canyon. Such warped rocks clearly evidence rapidly deposited layers that were still wet when they were bent.

"What is the point of today's message-closing lead-in? Just as the recorded history of Israel shows us, humanity began in an advanced state, regressed briefly into a primitive one, and then took 4,000 years to recover. But again, the foundation of Christianity rests on this planet's *God-revealed beginning*, which is its young earth age as opposed to the *theory* of evolution and its millions of years.

"Thank you for your presence here, today. Please think deeply about what God may have planted within you, and I look forward to sharing more with you tomorrow. But before we finish today, those who have been called to make a decision for Christ or who would simply like to talk with one of our pastors or associates, we will be here for as long as anyone wants to come forward. You come now. Just as you see others coming forward, you come, too."

HOT, COLD OR LUKEWARM

It was a bright and fresh day for the crusade's next broadcast messaging. On the way into the station Son-tu greeted several people she had seen a number of times on previous visits, but hadn't gotten to know any of them. To one, she smiled and said, "Good morning! It's a beautiful day to be alive." The person responded with a shrug. Son-tu stopped, held out her hand and said, "I don't believe we've actually met. My name is Son-tu. What is yours?"

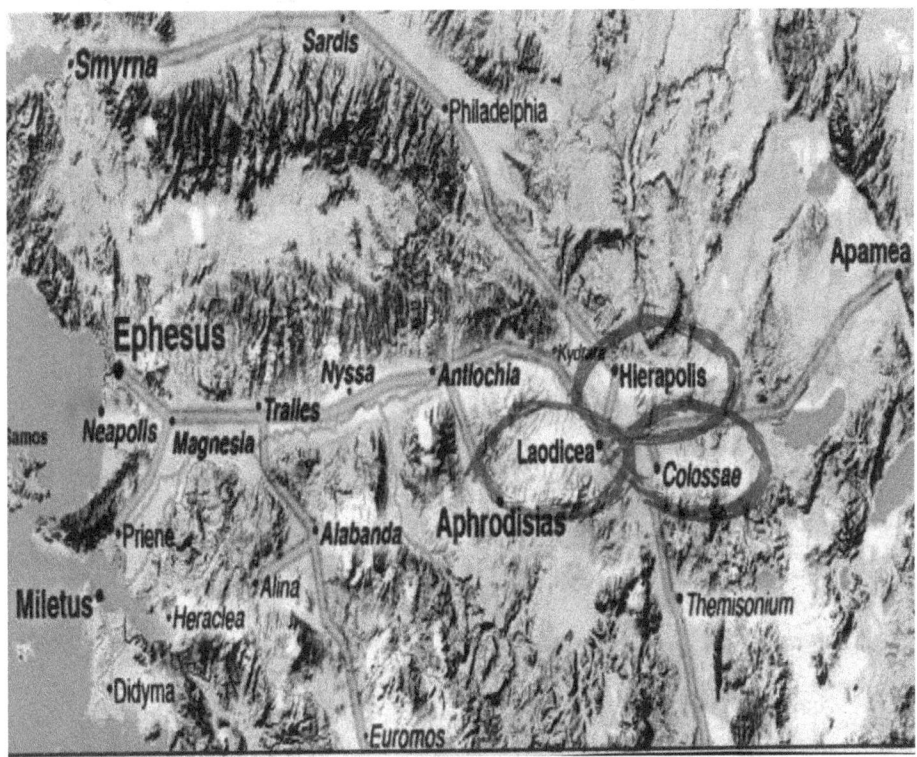

The church of Laodicea was the only one of the seven biblically mentioned churches whose people were noncommittal as to their spiritual belief in Christ. Translated, this means they were lukewarm in claiming to believe in Jesus, but were not truly regenerate believers. They had earthly goods, but had no spiritual flow.

By analogy, Laodicea had to import its water via aqueducts from elsewhere. Aqueducts brought hot water from the natural hot springs in Hierapolis and cold water from a fresh water spring in Colossae. By the time waters from both cities reached Laodicea, they were lukewarm, having lost the qualities that made them remarkable.

The woman nodded and said without expression, "I know who you are, I'm not a Christian, but have a good day."

Son-tu replied, "Well, thank you." *My goodness*, she thought, *what a perfect segue into today's message.*

Fifteen minutes later she was on-air. "What does the Holy Bible have to say about the immorality of infanticide? Let's start with this: What is wrong with a permissive society? And if there is no eternal God, surely there are no eternal principles of morality. Therefore, why not terminate an undesired or unplanned pregnancy? Who is really hurt if an unwanted child is never born? If humanity is not to be distinguished from the animal, why not live like an animal?

"In many societies today, half are for and half are against abortion. In terms of faith, Jesus called such general attitudes *lukewarm.* Let us digress for a few moments from my intended message for today to more closely examine the term *lukewarm.* In a book written many decades ago, its two authors (Richards and O'Brien) provide a very interesting take on the subject:

"Several miles northwest of Laodicea in Israel, perched on a small mountain, is a city called Hierapolis. At the base of the city is an extraordinary geological formation produced by the natural hot springs that surface around the city. Even today, Hierapolis is known for its steaming mineral baths.

"About the same distance from Laodicea in the opposite direction is Colossae. It was a less notable city, but it had one thing Laodicea didn't; a cold, freshwater spring. Unlike its two neighbors, Laodicea had no springs at all. It had to import its water via aqueduct from elsewhere: hot mineral water from Hierapolis and fresh cold water from Colossae. The trouble was, by the time the water from either city made it to Laodicea, it had lost the qualities that made it remarkable, i.e., the Laodiceans had nothing but *lukewarm* water.

"So, from this illustration, the Laodiceans probably understood the meaning of the LORD's warning to the Laodician Church as recorded in Rev. 3:15-16: *'I know your deeds, that you are neither cold nor hot. I wish you were either one or the other! So, because you are lukewarm—neither hot nor cold—I am about to spit you out of my mouth.'* In other words, Jesus wished His people were either hot for belief in Him, like the waters of Hierapolis, or cold in their lack of belief, like the waters of Colossae. Instead, their discipleship was unremarkable.

"You see the point of this illustration relative to abortion—that those who favor it have lost their way and see life as dirt cheap. In that regard the human race is like a blind man in a dark room looking for a black cat that isn't there. Unless the human race realizes it was created in the image of God—that people are individual beings and that they are accountable to their Creator—it will continue to sail its broken craft on a sea of despair and hopelessness, often unwilling to admit it has no map or compass for the journey. The pro-life goal has always been to make sure that unborn children are protected by law and welcomed in life. Abortion, on the other hand, is nothing more than infanticide.

"Now, on a broader note, I rely on the legendary Billy Graham—truly one of the evangelical giants of parts of the 20th and 21st centuries—in stating that the enormity of humanity's need is only heightened by the reality that a sure remedy is not only available, but free of charge. It is available for the reaching out and taking. However, with limited exceptions, most refuse to break the chains of pride that bind in acknowledging accountability to a higher Being.

"Continuing that evangelistic thinker's profound thread, God did not leave humanity to its own just desserts. Instead, the all-powerful Creator revealed His eternal plan of redemption, a plan so simple the most unlearned can *comprehend* it. It is also so profound the most educated cannot *exhaust* it. And it is so loving that eternity itself will not be sufficient to *proclaim* it.

"Beyond these three aspects it is literally so powerful no force in heaven—much less on Earth, Jun'or, or Andivoli—can *withstand* it. And lastly, it is so mysterious it would take a Lamb that will one day roar like a Lion to *unfold* it.

"If you would like to spend eternity in the presence of the Creator, get up and come down to one of the dozen or so well-marked mini-platforms and be helped today by one of our pastoral associates.

"Right now, friends, you get up and begin your walk to salvation and eternal life in Christ. Yes, you come right now while I am still speaking, because you may never again have this moment when you ache to scratch that interminable spiritual itch. You come now as you see others making their way to a new life through the LORD and Savior of humankind. Amen."

LATER THAT EVENING

When all the locally recruited support pastors and lay leaders had been briefly gathered to be thanked by Sontu, she said, "Thank all of you so much for your marvelous and selfless effort with planning and kicking off this crusade. Okay, that said, how do you think today went and what can we do better tomorrow?"

Boxx was the first to respond. "When we afterward demonstrated to those who came down how to also access hologram follow-up mentoring, the people invariably commented along the lines of; 'Wow!' or 'Perfect!' or some with even better comments such as 'I've always wondered about many things Christian' and 'Does this hologram-discipleship thing really work?'"

Boxx was fairly beaming at having shared that, and then added something even more specific: "One woman was particularly transparent, saying, 'I'm ashamed to say I have done some lamentable things in my life and I was afraid I had lost my salvation.' Seeing the opportunity to be a little more helpful, I demonstrated by showing her how to bring up that question-and-answer on her own com-glasses."

Boxx continued the testimony by actually bringing up Son-tu's hologram image in answering the person's question, which went thusly: "Thank you for asking this question. Such a person has not lost their salvation, but has broken his or her relationship with God. The solution to restoring that relationship is a matter of prayer and repentance."

He then nodded vigorously, adding that the woman had praised God and said she was greatly relieved. Finishing his lengthy input, he said, "We owe this incredible mentoring concept to you Bing-ta . . . and to your God-led guidance."

Bing-ta demurred, as always, saying, "Ah, thank you, kind sir. "I am but one tool in God's workshop. Without Son-tu's 'reacher-ship,' where would this project be?"

Son-tu thanked everyone, but quickly returned to the task at hand: "We have four more days to go. Does anyone else have an individual story to share?"

They did! The group went on for more than two hours before Son-tu reviewed the next day's schedule with them; also mentioning Vadim Jr.'s energetic and inspirational worship music line-up. Once Son-tu and Boxx were alone, however, he said, "I have to share with you something else. It is disquieting, to say the least, and I did not think it appropriate to share with the others."

Her expression betrayed her emotion as Boxx related the following: "The fellow I am now telling you about was not one of those who came forward at the invitation. Some minutes later, when people were exiting the area, he passed directly in front of me and I caught his thoughts."

"His *thoughts*?" Son-tu said, surprise in her voice. "So he had to be a Jun'orian!"

"Yes. I didn't have any reason to be tamping down potential telepathic receptivity since I didn't expect another Jun'orian presence here on Earth. What I got was this thought: '*The Andivolean woman equates the self-reproduction right of a female with infanticide! May she be damned unto Hell!*'"

Son-tu was shocked at the vileness of the thought, but she wanted to calm Boxx. "Not to worry. It is common enough for people to have strong thoughts without acting on them."

"I don't know," he said. "Where there is one such thought, there are likely to be more."

DAY TWO

Day two's live message was delivered similarly to the day before, other than with minor variations. Son-tu, however, did make a special effort to positively incorporate the context of several of the previous day's positive interactions. Boxx's concerns for Son-tu's safety, however, continued to fester and he met with Bing-ta about the Jun'orian thoughts he had gleaned.

Bing-ta was upset to hear the story and wanted to immediately hire a dozen security types. "No," Boxx adamantly replied. "We would have to advise her and she would not permit it. I know her and she would say, 'Are we not to trust in the LORD? Should we run scared of either shadows or giants?'"

With that, Bing-ta changed his tack. "Well, then whenever she is not on stage I am going to stick to her like Jordan River clay."

A tight-lipped Boxx replied, "Thank you, my friend, but I am more concerned for when she is *on* stage. For these final three days I am quietly going to see to having projectile-proof shields installed around the podium."

CRUSADE'S FINALE

Thankfully, days three and four proceeded uneventfully in terms of security concerns, but wonderfully relative to the messaging and the huge in-person audience. And that is without noting the wide-ranging, streaming audiences and Vadim's reformed New Jerusalem Band's energetic lead-in performance each day.

During the start of the fifth and final day of the Crusade, Boxx had been trying to target telepathic efforts toward the mind of the threatening-thought individual. Interestingly, he could sense that the target was aware of uninvited incoming thoughts, and was mentally steeling his thinking. *That's odd,* he thought, *unless that person had earlier been aware of another Jun'orian in the crowd having made a coincidental pick-up of his thoughts.*

He reviewed everything he and Bing-ta had done to ensure Son-tu's safety in the horrific event that the potential perpetrator might actually make an attempt on her life. They had erected 270-degree transparent projective shields around the podium. In addition, security agents were discretely scattered about the hillside, and the eyes and heightened senses of both Boxx and Bing-ta would be present on stage any time Son-tu appeared.

Son-tu was about to wrap things up for both the day's messages and the crusade itself. As always, her words were uplifting and personal. "Before I close what has been a wonderful experience for me—and I hope for many of you—let me reiterate a few things. I personally know the Creator is mindful of the crown jewel of his creation—all of humankind.

"He created everything that is, and He did it for us. Every human life, once conceived, is made in His image and thus is sacred. Anyone who is thirsty may come and drink of Christ's living waters and thus gain eternal life in His presence. May God continue to bless each and every one of you!"

At the precise moment of her final word a shot rang out and a physical body fell lifeless to the floor of the stage. Pandemonium broke out. There was instant shock and screaming, followed by disbelief and tears. Son-tu had fallen to the floor . . . not from being hit by a bullet, but from the surprise and horrific noise. Her mind was racing. *What has happened? Oh, my God, Boxx!*

She scrambled up and darted to where he lay on the stage, lying on his back. Bing-ta was already at his side. She had instant confirmation as to what had happened. Horrifying secondary thoughts struck her: *What was the threat Boxx gleaned from the wacko? 'The Andivolean woman equates the self-reproduction right of a female with infanticide. May she be damned to Hell!'* Her thought one second later: *He targeted Boxx to reach me!*

She could see he was bleeding profusely, but his eyes were focused on her. She couldn't speak and could barely see through her blinding tears. She softly called his name. He tried to speak but could only utter a few words: "You . . . did . . . well . . . darling. Until . . . we . . . meet .

. . again." With that, his head slumped forward, his body having lost life.

Late that evening, Son-tu visited a local church's chapel for prayer. Bing-ta was there and stood well back from her as she kneeled at the altar of one of the churches which had been founded by that of their missionary friend and guide from the U.S.A.

She was thanking God for the blessings of her husband and asking for guidance in going forward. "LORD," she softly intoned, "my husband has died twice. You once heard my plea for him to be given back his life on Jun'or and You miraculously reanimated him. This time, however, you have taken him safely home. Thank you, Father."

As she arose from her prayerful position, Bing-ta stepped forward and whispered her name. Taking her hand, they sat on a bench near the altar. Tenderly, he said, "Tell me more about my friend and your husband."

He could tell by her agonized expression that she was not capable of saying much, but her heart did allow her to wrench a few short sentences from her lips: "Thank you. I feel as far away from home at this moment than I have ever been. I once heard a line in a movie scene that has stuck with me ever since. It went like this: 'Marriage is a novel, not a short story.' That further reminds me of a relevant line from one of Boxx's favorite church hymns: '*One day I will see Him face-to-face . . . and tell the story saved by grace.*' Amen."

POST-MORTEM

"When and where do we begin again?" That was Bing-ta's sad question a week after Boxx's death and the crusade's end. He provided the eulogy, for which he dug deeper into himself more than he had since losing his wife. *Why was that,* he asked himself. *Because I will be speaking for an incredibly stoic woman who first lost her Christian mentor and paternal grandfather, and now her loving husband and partner.* Sadly, Boxx's and Son-tu's three estranged adult children would not be present.

He read much in preparation, including *The Voice of the Martyrs,* borrowing something about Christ being rightly esteemed in heaven, where the angels cry *Worthy is the Lamb!* He expanded on that note: "Scripture makes it clear that this is not the case in the fallen world, where our LORD is despised and rejected by men, essentially saying, 'We esteemed Him not' (Isaiah 53:3).

"But let me put this loss to you in yet other way," he said in speaking to those assembled. "You all know that the prophet Job (1:21) reminds us that *The Lord giveth and the Lord taketh away.* But in more Earthly phrasing, Queen Elizabeth the Second of England stoically said of Prince Phillip, when he passed away at age 99, 'Life consists of final partings as well as first meetings.'

"Every Christian is called to glorify God by working to ensure that Christ is known, loved and served by people from every tribe and nation. Finally, here today, what can be eminently said of Boxxton—a husband, a father, a friend, and a martyr—can be framed by a simple statement: Once he came to know Christ, he carried his faith as best he could, but it was too big, and he spilled it everywhere he went."

The day following the memorial service, and in a private room at the Kyiv police Chief's office, a grieving Son-tu was solemn in saying "the assassin certainly hit his target."

Bing-ta missed her point, saying, "You don't think the assassin was after *you*?"

"Oh, there is no doubt he was after *me*, but I was protected behind transparent, bullet-proof shields. The assassin, however, knew how to reach me where I *was* vulnerable . . . through my husband."

Bing-ta nodded. "Of course," he said.

The police Chief took the floor for a few things he wanted to share with the family. "Moments following the shot and in the process of securing the assassin, two security guards fatally shot the killer. A witness sitting two rows back and directly behind the killer said he heard the shooter say something as he turned slightly in his direction, while also spouting expletives. He quickly snapped together a three-piece rifle and took dead aim for the killing shot.

"Questioned here at the station," the Chief continued, "the witness gave his statement, prefacing it by saying that he is a writer and as such immediately committed the shooter's vile and evil phrase to memory. I will read to you what the witness said he heard: 'Death to those f-ing people who would deny a woman's absolute right to the use of her own body!' In other words, the assassin chose homicide to make his argument for infanticide! I have no doubt but what the killer's soul will suffer in Hell for eternity."

Both Bing-ta and Son-tu thanked the police chief and his team for all their help. "All I have to say at this time," Son-tu remarked as the two of them left, "is that God's judgment is good enough for me. Sadly, I must consider hardship as discipline. The Bible tells me that God's pruning process will allow me to bear more fruit." With a deep sigh amid tears, she added, "I want to go home to Jun'or, but first we have to return to Andivoli and see to the needs of the Alphas."

"The Alphas, of course," Bing-ta said in reminding himself. "Boxx loved them and liked to refer to Wy and Bea in that fashion."

As they walked out, Son-tu forced a smile and said, "You know, I'm so glad that you and he got along from the start because you will be able to remember him in some of the same contexts as you do me." For Bing-ta, her comment not only rang true, but he was glad he was spared by her not being able to read his deeper feelings.

LIFT-OFF

Telepathic communication between Son-tu on Earth and the Alphas on Andivoli had been brief for some time due to the press of the crusade. In addition, in the wake of Boxx's loss, Son-tu had not been up to allowing her emotions to flow freely in such an anticipated exchange. She did, however, finally express her intention to return to Andivoli in supporting Wy's and Bea's efforts, before they all headed back home to Jun'or.

"And Bing-ta?" Bea suspiciously inquired. "Will he be doing the same?"

"That is a good question. I have not yet inquired as to his plans."

A few days later the two were on their way to Andivoli. They had only been underway for several days when she broached the subject she had been pondering ever since Bea had posed her question: "What does the future hold for Andivoli's Fisherman/Evangelist?"

"Thank you for asking," he said, his eyes betraying more than mere interest in such a conversation. "I, too, have been giving much thought to that. You and Boxx brought me to an exciting new chapter in life. I am, of course, referring to the opportunity to make what little contribution I could to augmenting new believers' growth in their early faith. That alone greatly relieved my heretofore inordinate dependence upon my fishery business. But to see your personal life turned upside down while doing so much in serving the Creator and mankind . . . well, that is heartbreaking for me."

"Thank you, dear Bing-ta, but you have added greatly to two other lives as well. With time, new decisions come to everyone. So, each of us is now up against yet another change."

He had already made one decision and since he was not one to dance around a question mark, he grabbed ahold of it. "Listen, Son-tu, I have been aching to share some things with you. You know that I lost my wife to cancer, but there is more to the story. The cancer with which she was diagnosed was stage four. It was inoperable and therefore terminal. The doctors didn't say how long she might have, but my research suggested it might be a year or more."

Son-tu wondered where he was going with this, but she was more than merely interested in his story. "Tell me about it," she said.

"Thank you. We had brought all of our projects to a halt in order to simply live from one day to the next in enjoying our time together, praying thankfulness to God every day. She was not in acute pain, and except for two short hospital bouts, she remained at home under my care. She could not comfortably lie down because her damaged lungs would not allow her to breathe properly. A comfortably-padded and permanently-reclined arm chair with a foot stool would be her primary retreat for the rest of her life.

"What am I saying? During all those months we were not merely in *survival* mode, but *thriving*. I took her many places in town in her little electric scooter. It had two speeds, each marked with a rabbit and a turtle. Turtle was her speed and that was our lives.

"Here, then, is my point: My grief did not begin with her passing, as is your case with Boxx. You see, when my wife passed I had been grieving since her diagnosis nineteen months earlier. When she passed, I understood that had *I* been the one to pass I knew she would not have wanted me to endlessly grieve, but to get on with life. In other words, it is not what happens to a person, but what he or she does about it.

"Again, I fully realize that you have had no such lead time in dealing with your grief."

"Bing-ta," she replied, more than a little touched by his empathy, "I didn't know any of that. I am embarrassed that I . . . that is, Boxx and I . . . hadn't taken the time to learn more of your personal history."

"Not at all; after all, I could just as easily have enlightened the two of you. Nevertheless, all of that having been said, allow me to state my position. First off, please don't think me as too-forward in choosing to exercise a bit of text-proofing from the son of David's preaching in Ecclesiastes 4:9-11: *Two are better than one, because they have a good reward for their labor. For if they fall, one will lift up his companion. But woe to him who is alone when he falls, for he has no one to help him up. Again, if two lie down together, they will keep warm; But how can one be warm alone?*

"So you see, it is simple with me; I not only want to be a continuing part of your vision for helping others with the things of eternity, but if that should also come to include more of what lies before each of us, then that is what this Fisherman/Evangelist—someone who is falling in love with you—wants for his future."

She was momentarily left speechless. She had not been thinking in that direction, although she knew she was drawn to him. *Think, girl, think! No! This is too sudden.* "Bing-ta, I cannot, at this moment, offer a forthright response to your beautifully posited comments. I am at once overwhelmed, surprised, and thankful. Can we take a break for something a bit lighter?"

"Absolutely!" he said with a laugh. "As for me, that certainly beats a resounding 'No!'"

She blushed and said, "What I mean, kind sir, is that the craft's auto-pilot sensor just beeped a warning that Andivoli's orbital station is in range. What do you say to a verbal rematch with the central orbital station's wise guy-robot? You know; the one who named itself Mechanix after an eons-old illustrated mechanical magazine."

Bing-ta laughed, this time with serious humor. "I suspect that one of two things might have happened to it since our last visit: It may have either been promoted for its efficiency, or recycled to being a tomato juice can! That decision might well depend upon whether the Andivoli spaceport currently has a Human Relations Department or a Robot Salvage Section."

Neither her anticipation of their return to Andivoli nor his speculation concerning the future were answered because the subject of their disdain and discussion was simply not at its former post. Minus any robotic wisecracks, their entry would likely go smoothly . . . and did.

PART IV: ANDIVOLI RE-VISITED

CHECKING IN

Upon their arrival at the Alphas' camp, Son-tu instantly sensed there being a problem on the minds of both Wy and Bea. When asked, Bea addressed the nature of her stress: "Because of your terrible loss we didn't want to bring up our problem. As we have briefly communicated with you via telepathy, our church planting is going quite well. We have been blessed to have seen to the start-ups of six churches with pastors or laypeople who had already been home-churching small groups. We have added to their bases and have been sharing much and encouraging many. In other words, things had been looking bright . . . until several weeks ago."

Son-tu replied with, "Oh, my! Have you lost a critical leader?"

Wy and Bea looked at each other with faint smiles. "Quite the opposite," he began. "It all started shortly after your departure. I'm certain you recall the orbital receiving station robot you joked about before you left for Earth. Well, that bucket of bolts—now a supervisor—assigned another robot to visit our church. That 'bot reported that our mission might be supporting some kind of underground effort."

It was Son-tu's and Bing-ta's turn to look at each other. They did so while shaking their head. Wy confirmed what they were thinking. "Yes, we have six new *members*; all robots!"

Bea jumped back into the conversation, "Yes, and as you can well imagine, they are serious impediments to church development."

Son-tu surprised the Alphas with her response. "Not to worry! Look, allow me to back up to a time, decades ago, when I first showed up on Jun'or with grandfather Gam'man. The local authority there lost no time in assigning Boxx to us for the very reason you have just expressed. But when Boxx learned we weren't politically subversive he became our embedded ally."

"But that was different," Bea said with a contorted expression. "He wasn't a robot. These appliances are placed here to *find* governmental negatives. Surely we have to rid ourselves of them."

Now Bing-ta wanted a turn at the ever-developing robotic piñata. "If I may pose an analogy, think back with me to the Romans of Jesus' time! At first, they thought to rail against followers of 'The Way' because they feared the undermining of Caesar. But the Roman authorities soon came to believe that the rebels were nothing more than a Jewish cult. As a result they turned to simply disregarding them. That is, until the people began to hear people referring to Christ as some kind of King.

"My point is this: As was the case with Boxx's superiors, let's simply stay the course. In fact, I wonder if it might be possible to convert them. No, I didn't put that correctly. After all, they don't have beating hearts. Rather, I mean that if we politely and kindly enlist their help in furthering an understanding of Christian goodwill toward both men *and* robots, perhaps we can deflect their appointed animosity."

Son-tu seized on Bing-ta's last word. "That's it! All we need for the embedded robots to grasp is that they, too, do not have to perish . . . that is, so long as repair parts are available and maintenance is systemic."

At that, the four of them shared laughter.

SUPPORTING THE ANDIVOLI MISSION

Bing-ta was bringing the Alphas up to date. "We sent you an upload of the finished hologram-mentoring tutorial. Have you been able to implement it?"

"Good question," Wy replied, "but the answer is no. We have been focused on two other projects which seemed to take precedence: First, there is the recruitment of new believing members for the fledgling churches. Second, we are still in the process of trying to adapt to the six robots assigned to us by their celebrity supervisor, Citizen Mechanix."

Bing-ta nodded. "I understand. We want to help with both of those challenges. I like Son-tu's ideas concerning the robotic distraction, and I would very much like to help integrate the personal discipleship tutorial."

Later that same day, Son-tu sat down with Bea to discuss specifics of the individual church robotic assignments. Bea was anxious to share. "What is particularly interesting is the fact that each 'bot has a distinct personality. Not dramatically so, of course, but perceptibly. Of the six, the robot assigned to what we call the Home Church—the group which meets in our abode—seems to be a bit more empathetic."

"How do you mean?"

"Well, the first time it came to report on a church meeting, it arrived early. I was surprised when it asked if I needed any help to clean up the facility. There wasn't much in disarray so I asked what sort of help it could manage."

"It simply said, 'Whatever you can demonstrate for me.'"

"I decided to test it so I said, "We have a straight flight of wooden stairs leading up to the meeting room. Let's wipe down these stairs before our guests arrive." I wetted a mop and cleaned the first one before handing it over to the robot.

"It dutifully proceeded to mimic my mopping action, but only sloppily so. That's when I said, 'Not bad, but let me ask you an important question. I pointed to a corner and asked if it knew what that was called."

It looked at me and said, "Certainly. It is a 'corner'; a point where lines or surfaces join and form an angle."

"I replied, 'You are absolutely correct. In other words, a corner is not round. Why did you not clean the corner?'"

It bowed ever so slightly and said, "Your point is well taken. You asked me to clean the stairs and even demonstrated the process, but I failed to clean both of the two corners on each step. Corners are not round! I, robot, now know the truth of corners and will program myself for when I next clean stairs."

Bea turned to Son-tu and said, "You see what I mean?"

"That is fascinating! I want to meet it. And we have to do something about this name business."

The next evening began differently. "My name is Son-tu," she started a conversation with the Home Church's robot assignee. "Do you have a name?"

It hesitated before answering, "The title *Citizen* is common."

She shook her head. "But that is generic. It is common among our churches on Jun'or for participants to have individually distinctive names. For example, your own supervisor has a proper noun for a name. We would like to christen you 'Homey'. That's with a long 'o.'"

"What does 'christen' mean?"

"That simply refers to the first time a name is given to a body."

"Then call me 'Homey-with-a-long-o.'"

Son-tu successfully repressed a giggle. "We could, but we will call you by a shortened version in dropping the phrase, 'with a long o.' Do you understand?"

"I do. I am Homey."

"Now," Son-tu continued, "what is your relationship to the other five robots your supervisor has put in place with our Andivolean Mission home churches?"

"Nothing, except that on the rare occasion when they have a question for me. That is so because since I was the first *church* robot assignee it is presumed I have a singular memory experience."

"Excellent. And since you are first among our church home robots, we will call you Homey One, and each of the others—according to the order in which they were assigned—Homeys Two, Three, Four, Five and Six."

"I quite like that," Homey One said in activating an eye blink along with verbal confirmation: "I am Homey One. I will so communicate your preference to the other five."

FURTHERING DEVELOPMENTS

A full two weeks passed and Bing-ta had still not taken the time to re-develop a personal relationship with Wy, so he took advantage of an opportunity. "How do you think things are going now that we have been able to integrate the hologram tutorial with the various churches?"

Wy was happy to hear the question and launched into his answer. "Since re-focusing on that beautiful program, I find that it fits perfectly after having more actively demonstrated its workings. As you know, Bea and I rotate teaching among the various home churches, usually two locations per Sunday within a fifty mile range. We may have anywhere between thirty and forty in attendance at each location. Our broadcasts continue to attract new people as well, and we are also preparing a particular individual in each church to take over when we leave."

"Wonderful! And by the way, I have come to appreciate the term *mentoring* as an alternative to *discipleship*. What is your preference?"

"Um, I'm good with either. The tutorial is especially important from the perspective of it being an excellent support tool for the upcoming leaders. Until they can teach others to teach, how can they, themselves, be effective in teaching?" He paused before adding, "I like your idea of calling on several people at each session to post a relevant faith question through their com-glasses and then bring up the answering image on the room's larger screen for all to witness. Our success in doing that last night is the proof."

"Well done, my friend. Have you experienced any problems with the robots?"

"Not really, but we did with a human visitor. One fellow, apparently bent upon disruption, posed an odd pro-choice objection/question for which the tutorial had no answer. I handled it from the floor and after the service I addressed the subject with him in person. It didn't seem to change his mind and he hasn't returned to a gathering since, but I considered the instance a one-off."

That comment seemed to strike a particular chord with Bing-ta and he said, "Isn't it odd that the subject of abortion/infanticide seems to be more provocative in general than either creationism or salvation?"

"I know," Wy said with a nod. "That may be because it is simply more political."

A couple of days later, Son-tu had a second session with Homey One. "Homey," she began, "what personal questions do you have, aside from your responsibility for reporting any negative governmental or political statements made by any of the human leaders to which you are assigned?"

"Personal?" the robot replied with a head tilt suggesting curiosity.

"Yes. I know that all of our robots are fully able to read as well as converse, but I suspect the unique personality programming perhaps allows for a certain degree of curiosity about self. For example, I once heard your supervisor crack a joke at my expense."

Homey One double-blinked and said, "I have never before had anyone ask me a *personal* question. But yes, I do have a question. May I ask it?"

"Certainly!"

"I am familiar with most of my body parts and their manual function, but I am curious as to the word origin of one part in particular."

"And what part is that?"

"Motherboard."

Son-tu was taken aback. "That is a profound question, Homey One. Since you are not naturally familiar with the word 'mother,' you might not be programmed to know it can be used as a noun, a verb, or an adjective. Basically, the compound word 'motherboard' refers to something that holds and allows communication between crucial components of a system."

"Ah! So the 'board' in this compound word refers to some sort of physical computer surface on which some of my circuits would be mounted. I understand that. I am still curious, however, as to the 'mother' prefix, other than understanding the human birthing construct."

If Son-tu had been surprised by the first question, she was shocked by its follow-up question. "Homey, a mother is the origin or source of something. In your case I think it would simply refer to the sum of your manufactured circuits."

Homey pursued his line of questioning. "Humans have what is called a biological birth-mother. Do you recall your mother?"

At that question, Son-tu began to weep and emotionally waved off the robot.

Homey responded with, "I see that one of your body parts is not functioning properly. Perhaps I will ask again at another time."

That evening, Son-tu took Bea aside and said, "You know, my friend, I learned some things today from an unusual source. It made me realize that I have been way too steeped in myself of late. You aren't that much older than me. What are you missing most during this mission trip?"

Bea laughed and said, "Thank you for interjecting the adjective 'much.' I don't have to give that question much thought." With that, she sat down while patting the seat of the chair closest to her, "I miss Wy's and my home and our routine."

"Tell me about that."

"It's nothing special, but it is important. For example, simply taking care of the house and cooking for Wy and the occasional guest or family members."

"Cooking!" Son-tu exclaimed excitedly. What's your favorite dish?"

"Let me think. For Wy it would be anything sweet. But for me, I love to search com-glass recipes and try something that is either different or simply interesting."

"I like that. When Grandfather Gam'man and I first came to Jun'or I was into cooking for him. I didn't grow up with cooking lessons, but he had memorized a few recipes from his long-departed Earth wife, Lynn Michelson.

His favorite was a specially seasoned beef dish he called goulasch. When we get back to Jun'or I will cook it for you and Wy."

BROADCAST ENCORE

Son-tu managed a live, early morning broadcast on each of the next three days, with the station later repeating the broadcast three times on each of those days. On the fourth day she introduced herself as usual and then began her message with a bold question: "Thank you, Andivoleans, for tuning in to this sometimes controversial microwave band. Once again, this is your fellow citizen, Son-tu. As you know, I reside most of the time on Jun'or, but my crew and I are still fresh from a very successful evangelical tour on Earth. Hang on to your suspenders as I aim to challenge some of you, while hopefully reassuring others.

"Here's my question: 'Have *you* placed your faith in Jesus?' Then came her follow-up: "Okay, I know I'm not the first Christian 'reacher'—not to mention preacher or teacher—to be alarmed that many Christians sit within the Gospel net of thinking that they are saved because they have *named* the name of Christ, but don't *do* those things Jesus tells them.

"To put it even less delicately, they call LORD Jesus their God, but God isn't their LORD! In other words, they are hypocrites, making them false converts.

"Ok, don't try to get ahead of me. Let me tell you what scripture says about this: *And do you think this, O man, you who judge those practicing such things, and doing the same, that you will escape the judgment of God?* Yes, of one thing we may be certain: God's justice will be served. If anyone thinks he can escape God's justice on account of mercy, such would not be justice. Why? True mercy for

120

believers is the fact that God will not judge us according to what we *think* we deserve, but deliver us from the justice we *do* deserve."

She continued along that line for her allotted program time and closed, saying, "This has been the first delivery of the next-to-the-last day of my series of messages before my crew and I will be departing for our Jun'or home. We will, however, be leaving you in good hands. They are the local Christian leaders in the six new home churches at which many of you have joined. They are not only intent upon providing you with loving leadership, but also with a truly revolutionary resource for being personally mentored.

"Let me close this day's message by gratefully noting that the wonderful discipleship program to which I am referring was developed by one of your own—Bing-ta of the former fishery plant on our great Lake Andivoli. Take these paraphrased words from 1st Corinthians 15:2-4 to heart: *Continue to believe the Good News that Christ died for our sins and that He was raised from the dead on the third day, just as Scriptures said.*

INTERRUPTER

Just as the final day of the Andivoli re-visit was due to begin, Son-tu received word that the regional minister's office was requesting an appearance by her that afternoon. No explanation was offered other than the appointment time itself. She polled the other three as to what they thought might be the focus. The Alphas looked at one another with concern before Wy said, "Homey mentioned that its supervisor was expressing dissatisfaction with reports from all six of the mission's monitoring 'bots."

Son-tu turned to Bing-ta, frustration showing on her face, "That would be the work of our ever-hostile robot, Mechanix. Why don't you see what more you can learn from Homey One. I have to deliver my morning's broadcast."

Having said that, she also realized something else: "Oh, boy! Wouldn't you know that my message will also be dealing heads-up with creationism versus evolution." Putting her forefinger to her chin she noted aloud, "I know I've said this before, but it's time to say it again: "Ours is not merely to charge the summit, but to hold it." She then took a deep breath before making yet one more decision: "Heck, I have another couple of gospel grenades I can throw into the flames this morning. They have to do with the sorry evolution of AI into human affairs."

Bing-ta said, "Hear! Hear! But, dear, don't cause us to either lose sight of our broader redemption message or our likely need to mount a premature departure."

Son-tu's cue to begin came from a red-eyed camera 'bot which did something with one of its *eyes* that resembled a wink: "Good morning all you Creator-loved people who either believe in the concept of eternal life in His presence, or are *coming* to believe. Isn't it incredible that mankind in general will go to such great lengths to avoid worshipping his or her Creator God.

"I mean that this world tends to either bow down before 'Mother Andivoli' or 'Father Time,' or even to the robotic result of progressive AI." With that remark she didn't think she had yet damaged the mission group's cause but she was pretty confident she was wearing their welcome thinner than even before. *How can I clean this up a bit?*

"Okay, faithful listeners, allow me to expand. Why do most people still believe in evolution? Frankly, there is a simple answer to that question. It was perhaps first stated by Earth's John Morris in a book in 1994 when he wrote, 'Most people believe in evolution because most people believe in evolution.' That is more profound than you might think. Why? Because that's all they have ever been taught! If creation is even mentioned in schools or by the media, it is ridiculed and unfairly caricatured. Thus, evolution is assumed but not proved, and creation is denied but not proven wrong.

"Beyond that, we must get away from thinking of evolution as a science. The *theory* of evolution is a philosophical world-view about the past, which presently exists. It is a frantic attempt to explain the fact that mankind is here without a Creator God. May God grant *this* planet, Andivoli, a return to light and logic before it is too late."

A few hours later Son-tu was sitting in the office of the regional minister, screening her thoughts from the pompous Andivolean hiding behind a ridiculously large desk. Beside him was seated one of his robotic supervisors.

"Madam Son-tu," the human began, "Citizen Mechanix here tells me that you and your off-planet crew . . ."

Son-tu stopped him in mid-sentence, saying, "Pardon me, Minister, but both Bing-ta and I were citizens of Andivoli before Mechanix was anything but scrap metal."

The minister did not care for that comment and said, "Now that is what we used to refer to as blatantly defamatory language. As I was about to say before you interrupted me, your crew has managed to either corrupt or insult every aspect of Andivoli society, including our governmental robotic entities. That is against Andivolean law, whether by citizens or non-citizens."

"Sir, *insulted*, I understand, but *corrupted*, how so?"

"Well," he stammered a bit in turning to glance at the robotic aide as he continued his accusations, "the units which report to Citizen Mechanix have not been forthcoming with substantive reports of you and your followers' surely unlawful statements and conduct."

"Would the minister mind defining 'substantive'?"

The minister raised a forefinger without actually speaking. He then turned to his robotic aide, nodding for it to answer the question. "Thank you, sir," Mechanix began with an awkward impression of a smile, "that word means 'dealing with essentials.'"

The minister frowned and said, "You idiot! What *are* the essentials?"

"The essentials are the lack of reporting anything substantive."

Son-tu was suddenly enjoying the interview. "Oh, now I understand," she said. "You are using circular reasoning for your charge of the lack of anything resembling negative aspersions regarding the government."

"Yes, that is it precisely," Mechanix replied.

"That's enough, 'bot!" said the exasperated minister.

"Look, citizen Son-tu," the minister re-started in attempting to take back the authority he had abdicated, "you have been both impertinent and disruptive since you and your counterparts first arrived. I heard your broadcast earlier today and your railing against some of the people's common beliefs, not to mention your obvious prejudice against AI and robots. I am herewith replacing all six of the servicing robots at your little churches, *and* deporting the two of you, along with your two hirelings. You have 24 hours to leave Andivoli!" He was so proud of himself that if Mechanix were not a robot he would have either high-fived or fist-bumped it in his exuberance.

As the pair departed the building, Bing-ta chuckled before saying, "As one of Earth's long-ago humorous life's commentators once quipped, 'Computers can never completely replace humans. They may become capable of artificial intelligence, but they will never master real stupidity.'"

PARTING WITNESS

Son-tu shared the interview's relevant points with the Alphas, to which she added, "I'm going to fire a parting broadcast shot yet today, so be ready immediately afterward to board the *Boundless* for our planetary exit."

"Welcome back, faithful audience," she began. "This will be my final broadcast until such time as we return to Andivoli. Here is my question for today: 'What is the greatest atrocity to be inflicted upon mankind?

"As horrific and shameful as is some of our mother planet Earth's history, including slavery, I agree with one insightful writer's comment that 'it is minuscule in comparison to the unjust, immoral, shameful and horrific practice and/or indifference to the murder of countless young Andivolean children prior to an exit from the womb.' Yes, abortion is no kind of solution to human brokenness and pain. What we *do* need are men and women to commit to their children—allowing their own family to be a witness to life.

"It is a fact that infanticide is the leading cause of regressive population on this planet! Multiple administrations and its supposedly representative lawgiving bodies have had to resort to manufacturing robots to properly populate the needed workforce.

"It is a sad enough circumstance for Andivoli to be struggling with staying ahead of deaths outnumbering living births, but it has also allowed itself to yield to Satanic influences in the past by combining human abductions from Jun'or and Earth with Andivolean donor eggs, effectively yielding bastard babies.

"Let me put this into proper context: Recall that the founding colony of this planet, along with the Andivolean Declaration of Independence, intended to portray an ideology of a government which protects those who are most vulnerable and unable to defend themselves.

"Instead of that, what we have had for more than forty years is the continuation of a fatally degraded planet. Will Andivoli never put forth the leadership necessary for its survival? Even today, our own small crew finds itself being deported for having tried to make a difference. We pray there are some who will rise up and heed the call. *You* may be one of those!"

PART V: RETURN TO JUN'OR

LIFT-OFF

Immediately following delivery of Son-tu's message, the foursome conducted a hurried look around their short-term housing facility and then dashed to the holding dock of the *Boundless*. Also in that process was the matter of ignoring several recorded *imperative* messages from Son-tu's regional minister nemesis.

With Son-tu serving as pilot, she quickly put the necessary coordinates for their flight to Jun'or into the ship's computer. Bing-ta had foreseen the sudden departure several days earlier and had seen to quarter-mastering the compact spacecraft's necessary supplies as well as Son-tu's and his shipboard needs. He also advised the Alphas to see to their personal needs . . . and then he saw to one other special item.

He not only liquidated his significant holdings in his fishery business on Lake Andivoli, but signed over ownership of his house to the First Homey Church. The only material possession he did not dispose of in some way was the small sailboat he and his late wife had once used for a trip involving the repeating of their marriage vows. He told the dry-dock manager that he might someday return to Andivoli for a visit.

The Alphas were so excited about "going home" that no sooner had they boarded their craft but what they began plying Son-tu with trip-relevant questions. Bea said, "I think it took us ten days to make the outbound jump. Any chance we can cut that down some?"

Son-tu looked at her, and with a sly expression said, "Bea, I'm surprised at you. You mean you want me to cut a corner?"

All Bea could do in reply was to say, "Busted!"

Wy didn't know what to make of all that and so he put up a hand to signify restraint. "Do you realize, dear wife of mine," he now tried to good-naturedly lecture her, "that this is a trip half-way across the galaxy, and that without our little craft's marvelous hyper-space drive we would otherwise arrive at our beloved Jun'or at about the same time your beautiful locks would turn white?"

"Dear husband of mine," she said, "you are selling past the sale. I have already bought in."

"Okay, gentle folk," Son-tu interjected, "fasten your seatbelts. We will be lifting off within fifteen minutes. Then, once we are advancing well toward the perigee for our hyper-space jump, we can settle in. Perhaps the Alphas would then share something with Bing-ta and me as to some of their particularly enlightening recent experiences with the Homey One congregation."

Wy saw opportunity for a momentary diversion before sharing something relevant to the commencement of their starry mission's return home. He stood up with one palm also up and said, "Sit back and relax folks, and thanks for traveling with us. We know you have other choices!"

That brought a three-person chorus of boos. Ignoring their boorishness, he continued. "Back to the request, no sooner had I begun one of my evening messages and uttered the phrase, 'The Heavens declare God's glory,' but what I was interrupted—actually 'graced' might be the better word—with this: 'In what way, pastor," the questioner said, "do the heavens declare God's glory?' I won't regale you with the whole story I then related, but here are the Cliff Notes I memorized years ago from its author, the Jewish founder and President Emeritus of a very successful Bible-based ministry on Earth:

"First, the heavens reveal His *existence*; and as such creation requires a Creator. Second, the heavens reveal

His *wisdom*; design requires a Designer. Third, they reveal His *power*, movement requires a Mover. And fourth, since the universe is endless, the heavens reveal God's *infiniteness*."

The threesome nodded appreciation, but Wy had only begun. "Another way in which the heavens declare God's glory is that the many lessons God provides to show how His justice works—that is, for man's sins to be forgiven—blood had to be shed. Now the believer is in a unique position to be a vessel fit for the Master's use, and here is how that plays out: At Calvary, grace and truth kissed. That means that the holiness of God was eternally satisfied, and the believer, having experienced those attitudes firsthand at the cross, is to reflect the character of his God to the world.

"Now finally," Wy said in closing his monologue, "how do you think this minister I am quoting landed that message's plane? Well, he did so with this elegant sentence: 'Humanity has been afforded the incomparable privilege of demonstrating with their lives and proclaiming with their lips the intrinsic, eternal, perfections of God—of glorifying Him and enjoying Him forever.'"

None of the other three had so as much as shifted position during Wy's brief re-cap of his message. When he finished, however, Son-tu attempted to stand to congratulate him. In so doing, she bumped her head on the overhead rack, wincing in the process, Bea and Bing-ta, seeing the result of Son-tu's effort, settled for a less demonstrative response by remaining seated while clapping and calling out, "Amen and Amen!"

LANDING THE *BOUNDLESS*

The crew was on its final day of the ten-day hyperjump and all four were eager to remove themselves from the smallish confines of the craft's four hammock-style cubicles. After all, it only had one common area other than the "rest" facility. Jun'or did not possess orbital reception stations as did Earth and Andivoli. Son-tu called up the computerized guidance/landing program and put in the desired coordinates, along with the necessary authorization ID and retinal scan before skillfully setting into play the craft's auto-docking procedure.

The craft's gravity-controlled descent onto the assigned space travel pad had precisely progressed and everyone was now safely on Jun'or firma, waiting for surface transportation. They still had to run the gamut of planetary customs, however, but official Prior and Proper Authentication had been seen to upon entering Jun'or's final-orbital approach.

With the crew's home port landing, the Mission to Mankind tour officially ended. Wy and Bea returned to their family and their departmental work at Gam'man University. Son-tu went directly to her combination home and ministry headquarters, but not before seeing to proper lodging for Bing-ta in a different wing. As she was showing him around he said, "We need to talk."

She smiled, and with both of her hands she playfully bent her ears forward while saying, "As you can see, I'm all ears."

"Okay. Sit, girl, sit! On the way over you asked about my future plans. I have Plans A and B. If A does not seem feasible, Plan B will be for me to return to Andivoli and take back my life in the fishery business."

At that, Son-tu expressed wide-eyed surprise. "But you just shared with us that you have given away your home and sold your business!"

"Then I must be counting on Plan A!"

"And what is Plan A, my dear Fisherman-Evangelist?"

"It picks up from where we left off before landing on Andivoli. Out of full disclosure, I have been envious of friend Boxx from the first time you and I met in-person. When I lost my first wife to cancer, a good friend and Christian pastor shared an old saying with me. It goes like this: 'As a believer's dear one leaves us in this life and we sadly say, 'There he goes,' at the same time others in heaven are brightly saying, 'Here he comes.'

"My point is this: As saddened as I was by Boxx's loss, and as profound as I know is your loss, I nevertheless restate my having fallen in love with you. Now, let me add that if you are not yet in a reciprocal position, but are willing to encourage me, I will remain here for a time as a suitor." At that, he stopped and said, "You know something; that was pathetic! I am going to let you off this hook by saying, why don't we first get ourselves grounded and then I will do this right. I know you well enough, dear Son-tu, to know that then you will not long dally in making a decision."

The intended said to herself, *I was not expecting this . . . but why not, you idiot? He has been dealing all of his cards face up from the first time we met. You have been telling yourself you can be strong without the 'helper' God told the first man was needed in life, and you have certainly told others in similar situations that the Creator did not write that lesson merely for Adam's benefit. Be honest with him!*

"Perhaps I should have known this was coming, but I didn't. I, too, am pathetic in that respect. Your willingness to be vulnerable is yet another remarkable thing, my Bing-ta. Give me a bit more time before likely advising you to cancel that one-way ticket to Andivoli!"

HITCH IN THE GIDDY-UP

Two weeks later, things had begun settling down for the Chessers and for Son-tu and Bing-ta. Gam'man University's chairman of the board, Georgi Washington, had communicated with Son-tu the day before in asking if she and Bing-ta would visit him at his GU office about a delicate matter. They were both quite busy, but agreed to come.

The two of them arrived on campus early in order for Bing-ta to take a first-time tour of the campus. An hour later they were in the Chairman's office, being warmly greeted by him, along with repeating his congratulations for the mission's success, including Bing-ta's revolutionary evangelical tutorial hologram project. Following that he came to the primary point of his request, but a bit awkwardly, or so it seemed to Son-tu. It would not take long for her to understand why.

"Here we go," he said. "The Board is suffering from some infighting headed by a name Son-tu knows very well—Master Sloann!"

"What?" she said, aghast. "You surely don't mean a Sloann descendant of my grandfather's arch antagonist from Earth!"

"Precisely! It is the atheist grandson, who now lives on Jun'or. Let me explain and then I will share with you why I have asked you to visit. When this school first offered graduate programs and thus became a university—greatly helped by Son-tu's grandfather's contributions—it was also renamed in his honor.

"During the time of your recent mission, the board received—and approved— a very large donation to our building fund for needed student housing. At the time, I wasn't familiar with the donor's organizational name, but all of the financial boxes were checked. On the day of

132

closing, the donor's representative mentioned that he understood there was a precedent for GU to award a board position to someone making a contribution of such size, and he asked for that appointment to be given to his client, the donor.

"I was surprised by that statement," the chairman continued, "but in checking our financial archives I learned that that very thing had been done for Son-tu's grandfather. Given that precedent the board could hardly do other than approve. He is now quite literally both on the board and aboard, pun not intended.

"So, all of that is but a lead-in to several other items relevant to the purpose of my asking for your visit. First of all, Son-tu, Gam'man University has special need of your increasing visibility and influence."

She wrinkled her nose and said, "Chairman Washington, you know that whatever is in my power to do for this university will certainly be accorded."

The chairman chuckled. "Well-framed, my dear! First of all, everyone at GU is greatly saddened by your tragic loss of Boxx. The prince of our worlds continues his evil rein over much in this life, but you and your team's recent successful evangelical mission with its many remarkable exploits have been another testimony to the Creator's continuing grace, providence, and hope for humanity."

"That is over the top, Mr. Chairman, and I/we thank you, but now I believe you are coming to the specific purpose of your request for our visit."

The chairman nodded, saying, "You are one after my own management philosophy concerning pressing forward in achieving objectives: And my use of the word *philosophy*, though unintended, is relevant. First off, as you know, we currently have a combination department of Religion and Philosophy at GU. In addition, I am adding a new, separate department: the Department of Faith. Why? Christianity is not a religion, but a belief and divine faith in Christ alone. I consider the combined general study of humanity's philosophies and religions—past and present—to be outside of true Christian faith. With your concurrence, I want to appoint Wy and Bea Chesser as co-heads of the Department of Faith."

Son-tu's eyes lit up to a new level of brightness. "That is wonderful news, Mr. Chairman, and as my grandfather might have said, 'I am sure that will be no step for dancers!' Thank you for sharing this with me. I can hardly wait to congratulate them." Then, with a suspicious grin, she said, "That, however, was not much of a favor to ask."

Again, the chairman smiled, but this time he was about to become totally transparent. "There is much more. The President of GU has this week announced to the board his retirement. You may have known something of that possibility. In any event, what we need is someone with organizational business experience, proven leadership, and a commitment to Christian values."

With that, the chairman turned to look directly at Bing-ta. "Even though you, sir, have yet to apply for Jun'orian citizenship, I'm certain that will not be a problem. I also have every belief that you are not only committed to the required values called for by this position, but that you have the ability to adapt to GU needs. That said, Bing-ta, I am offering you the presidency of Gam'man University."

Son-tu was even more radiant in her response to this second announcement. Before he had a chance to respond, she hugged the surprised Bing-ta and said, "Well now, honey, I believe you can stop working on your résumé." Turning to the chairman she said, "So that is why you insisted on bringing Bing-ta with me!"

"Not entirely. I still haven't fully asked my favors. Because of the Christian threat recently revealed by Sloann, dear Son-tu, we need you on the board, along with Bing-ta. You have been invited to join it in the past, but you have always demurred due to your evangelistic commitment. I must also mention, however, that I suspect Sloann's agenda surely includes some sort of motivation that does not bode well for the family which contributed to the demise of both his evil grandfather and father.

"Now, if the two of you will grant us these appointments the university is also prepared to provide your ministry with a grant of one million Jun'orian units for the purpose of Christian evangelism."

Son-tu's radiance bulb was about to burst. She and Bing-ta stood as one, glanced at each other, and then nearly simultaneously said, "I do!"

NEW RESPONSIBILITIES AND CHALLENGES

Another two weeks passed and with it several special events took place. Bing-ta became a naturalized citizen of Jun'or while continuing to hold dual citizenship on Andivoli. Following that he was installed at GU's new President.

The Chessers had settled in with having quickly taken co-headship of GU's newly created Department of Faith. They, in turn, enthusiastically advanced Johnni's and Pyoter's temporary Jun'or Evangelical Mission leadership to full authority.

The university's first board meeting took place after both Son-tu and Bing-ta had been formally installed. With removal of the former president's left-leaning cultural and political perspectives in favor of Bing-ta's conservative administrative leadership and the addition of Son-tu's seat, the board votes had swung from five to four in favor of liberals to six to three in favor of conservatives.

Next up was the first brief meeting between Son-tu and Sloann III. Unlike his family predecessors, Sloan presented himself as a middle-of-roader, personally voicing "wherever possible" conciliation with his counterparts. There was no mention of family histories.

It wasn't long, however, before an anonymous spoiler made public headlines in countering one of Johnni's and Pyoter's Rimerian media statements on the subject of abortion. The subject of that headline was not on the university board's monthly meeting agenda, but Sloann brought it up during the "new business" segment. "It seems to me," he began, "that the age-old argument for and against a woman's right to health decisions involving her own body should at least be granted a voice."

Chairman Washington was concerned by the statement and addressed it. "Since you brought it up, Master Sloann—and to use your own logic—why would an unborn baby not also have a right to an advocate for a decision involving his or her body? Since that subject is not germane to today's agenda, we will not be addressing it further."

The Rimerian Movement, however, would shortly counter the unsigned public opinion column's argument. Authored under the names of Johnni and Pyoter, their article took the headline of *Justifications Offered for Committing Abortion*. In it, the Ruter Critique was quoted and picked up by several of the planet's largest platform publishers. Bing-ta saw it and read its closing paragraph aloud at a regular meeting called for the benefit of all GU's department heads:

"The premises for justifying abortion/infanticide are absurd. To say that a child does not become a human being until it nears the time of delivery from a mother's womb defies both science and truth. To reject the God-given right of a citizen to pursue its life to natural conclusion purely for the protection of another person's choice to end that life is absurd. Beyond that, a sane individual cannot participate in such atrocities acted toward another individual without being scarred and damaged emotionally and psychologically." That was the end of it in terms of the GU board.

Several more weeks passed and a political group openly funded by Sloann's left-leaning interests, wrote a published opinion column by a candidate running for regional minister. Its subject, however, took a surprising end run in pushing its perspective on a very different subject; the never-ending controversy about the mystery of life's origins. The article's focus was thus: "We reject as backwards and superstitious the orthodox Christian belief in a personal God and the natural law, the same way that orthodox Christians once rejected paganism."

After reading the full article, Son-tu took the opportunity to rhetorically ask her confidants a question: "Why do so many people predictably persist in their acceptance of some version of chemical evolution?"

She then shared how imaginatively the opinion writer had answered that particular question: "Chemical evolution has not been *falsified*. In a strict, technical and scientific sense, chemical evolution *cannot* be falsified because it is not falsifiable. This is a speculative reconstruction of a unique past event, and cannot therefore be tested against recurring nature. Pro-lifers would thus impose upon women forced birth and unchosen obligations."

Son-tu wrote an opinion letter of her own, commenting on the initiating writer's remarks: "A part of life includes potential burdens and dangers of parenthood and pregnancy along with unchosen obligations and legal and moral duties. Those who cannot accept the accountability owed a Creator will never cease their efforts in denial." Then, it occurred to her to add a further balancing thought: "Surely, pregnancy is not the woman's responsibility alone. Don't let dads walk. By that, I mean how about the idea of legislation compelling child support just after conception?"

PROVOST

Mirrored silhouette is suggestive of invisible printed text on a whiteboard which Sloann's chemical process nevertheless provided its words to register on viewers' minds.

One day, not long after some of the public argumentative barrage concerning abortion and infanticide, evolution versus creationism, and salvation through faith in Christ alone had settled down, a strange subject was suddenly brought to light. Within days it had come up in all the media.

An anonymous article asserted that according to records stored in Gam'man University's archives, when the original school was chartered as a college in honor of Jun'or's champion evangelist, Gam'man, he had been given the posthumous title of Provost, which was defined as 'Head Administrator of Gam'man College.'

That is the point at which the article's intrigue began. Apparently, due to some archaic Jun'orian legal language: "The posthumous Provost title of any organization remains in perpetuity and can even come to be held by a living person, provided he/she be duly elected." The article's anticlimactic point was that anyone can run for such position provided there be a call for an election. The article ended with this quote: "I, the discoverer of this historical legal covenant—but wishing to remain anonymous—hereby nominate our own national heroine, Son-tu, to run for official GU Provost."

When the board learned of the article and proceeded to verify its lawfulness, Chairman Washington said, "However quaint this situation, it is legal, thus we must call for an election by the public of this local civil division, with Son-tu as the nominee."

The chairman's administrative assistant, present at that meeting, raised her hand, saying, "Point of Order, sir. Might there be other nominees?"

Surprised, but understanding her point, he said, "I suppose we have to allow that, but I don't think it has to be stated. After all," he smiled in adding, "who would be nominated to run against our founder's granddaughter?" All those present, laughed, except for Son-tu.

Over the coming days, special election processes took place and 25,000 people of the voting district went to the polls. There were three names on the ballot, one of which was known by all to be someone who routinely but unsuccessfully ran for everything from city council to governor. Son-tu's name, of course, was on the ballot, along with one totally unanticipated name . . . Sloann III!

How did the vote go? Shockingly, Sloann won with more than 50-percent of the total vote, which meant there would be no run-off.

Chairman Washington was quick to air his concern at the hastily called board meeting, minus an uninvited Sloann. "Do you realize that the Provost title is equal to or superior to Board Chairman? How could this possibly happen?! I mean, he didn't even mount an advertising campaign, just as was the case with Son-tu. Well, other than his in-person interviews . . . of which, however, I now realize, there were a great many."

Son-tu stood, and, in her even-toned fashion, said "I have two thoughts on what just happened. The first is a tired cliché quoted by Boris Johnson, the British Prime Minister in 2022 who, upon being forced to resign, said, 'Them's the breaks!'"

"My second thought, however, is that there is another way in which this could have happened. Here is my theory: This takes advantage of the fact that the mind is capable of registering information outside of awareness. A special application of this concept was invented by Sloann's paternal grandfather.

"The concept was once publicly proven via Sloann-the-first's Mirror Magic firm on Earth more than half a century ago. How do I know? My grandfather, Gam'man, and I, with the help of others, including Wy Chesser's grandfather, exposed the scheme and took it down."

The Chairman was frowning. "Please expand a bit further on the process itself."

"All Jun'orians know about the curse of mental telepathy; that given the lack of an active and directed mental defense, any Jun'orian who is at least a half-blood—which is my case—can receive another Jun'orian's directed thoughts. This has apparently been a Jun'orian curse since mankind's rebellion against God in geo-

colonizing Jun'or. Mental telepathy is a learned adaptation of ESP which allows the potential for initiative to be maximized."

Bing-ta was anxious to interject a comment. "Since I am neither Jun'orian nor even cognizant of the workings of the process of mental telepathy, share with us how Sloann could utilize that to his advantage."

Son-tu looked around to see nothing but heads nodding. "Okay! First off, subconscious effects can occur in the *absence* of conscious effects, meaning that subliminal stimulation can otherwise enter the mind unnoticed, that is, without conscious awareness. It should be noted, however, that with unconscious perception of stimuli, only simple or compelling signals are received. In other words, one could not register on someone else's mind Lincoln's *Gettysburg Address*."

The Chairman ran a hand through his hair. "But what would have been his opportunity for delivery?"

"I have given that a great deal of thought. Think about his seemingly endless interviews! What was particularly different about his many interviews versus my few?" Then, in a frivolous aside, she said, "I mean, aside from his points not being substantive." Mild laughter ensued.

Then, Bing-ta's head snapped up and he said, "Hey, there was one thing he always did that everyone thought was merely quaint. Remember him holding up a rectangular piece of white board—maybe 45mm x 15mm—with five bold words which read, 'For WHOM should I vote?' as he amusingly pointed to himself. When questioned about it by interviewers he always joked about wanting to reach both the audibly challenged and those who routinely muted commercials and political messaging."

Son-tu gave Bing-ta the universal *thumb's up* sign, while barely avoiding use of the colloquial phrase, 'Bingo!' To that she excitedly added, "Yes! I hadn't made anything of it either, until now. Your point also brings something else to mind. One long-ago study on Earth showed that if there is 'spare capacity' in terms of an observer's attention to whatever he or she is reading or watching, the brain will allocate that resource to subliminal activity."

She had hold of a thread she would not release until it was fully unwound. "Consider this: In addition to his message board's few, bold and simple visibly-printed words of question, Sloann could theoretically *invisibly* include another three or so subliminal lines, either above or below the visible words, which might read something like this: 'For SLOANN should I vote!' Sloann's grandfather had the chemical formula to invisibly execute something exactly like that. In fact, he did so using mirrors rather than a white board."

"But that's illegal!" several of those present declared, nearly in unison.

Son-tu winked. "As the cliché goes, 'Crime doesn't take holidays.' Neither do the Sloanns. Far more importantly, since this speculation couldn't be proven in court, what do you suppose Sloann might possibly have in mind beyond merely being elected GU Provost? Fifty years ago—with this very concept—the older Sloann not only accomplished his advertising business coup in turning Mirror Magic into the largest ad agency on Earth, but it also positioned him for a run for President of the United States. Had not the aforementioned opposing forces been able to sabotage Sloann's gamble into the loss of both his enterprise and his life, it's hard to know what could have happened."

Terry Dodd

WHAT TO DO?

The next day saw a specially-called committee meeting made up of Chairman Washington, Son-tu, Bing-ta, and the Alphas. The Chairman's hands were wet with sweat. "Aside from a few would-be activist Christians who have suggested on Jun'or social media that Sloann should be introduced to kiln-fire temperatures, we need to realistically address his likely covert—if not *overt*—threat to GU and beyond."

Wy and Bea had expressed particular interest in sharing several perspectives on the subject. Bea was sitting close to the edge of her chair and quickly raised her hand. "Mr. Chairman, did Sloann not sign a Statement of Christian faith when he accepted a board appointment, even though I understand he essentially bought his seat?"

The Chairman nodded unenthusiastically. "You are correct on both points, but even if he were to be asked point-blank if he believes salvation involves the redemption of the whole man or woman and that it is offered freely to all who accept , he would probably say, 'Where do you want me to sign?' In other words, now that he knows his operating method for much greater rewards in this life works, I doubt his conscience is going to be concerned with the next life."

Wy's itch, too, had yet to be scratched. He figuratively tipped his hat to his wife before launching an idea. "I suggest we stir up public resentment of him by letting Dietrich Bonhoeffer's words call him out. Then we can mount a Christian offensive through the public."

From Wy's unfiltered thoughts Son-tu instantly knew to what he was referring. "That," she said, "is an interesting idea. Through opinion columns and ads we try him before the public by crowning him the king of 'cheap grace.'"

Bing-ta was eager to jump onto the rolling wagon. "Ah, one of my favorite subjects and theologians: Bonhoeffer tells us that cheap grace is the grace we bestow upon ourselves, that is, grace without discipleship; whereas, *costly* grace is the gospel which must be sought again and again; the gift which must be asked for; the door to which a man or woman must be familiar."

Only Chairman Washington had not so far cast his lot on the subject. "You folks are truly preaching it. People often ask why it is called costly. I love telling them it is costly because it costs a man his life. And it is grace because it gives a man the only true life. Sadly, some in-name-only Christians proclaim that Christ is worthy *only* if He benefits us, and certainly not if He *costs* us. So, ladies and gentlemen, I propose we reveal Sloann as a cheat, a liar, and someone unworthy of directing anything Christian."

Son-tu was proud of the team's enthusiasm for addressing the problem, and so turned to Bing-ta with a question: "What is our next step, Mr. President?"

Surprised, but prepared, he replied, "We begin tomorrow. I will present him with a public document asking for his resignation from GU as both Provost and a board member, and that he is being sued for fraudulent statements made on a legal document."

Georgi Washington was sold, saying, "Perfect! Of course he will reject all of it and no doubt counter with a lawsuit; perhaps even appealing to the court of public opinion himself, based on his financial contributions to scholarships, public housing, student debt payoffs, and anything else that appeals to voters at the polls."

"Let him!" Son-tu said, effectively adjourning the meeting. "Frankly, without cheating, I don't think he could be elected dog catcher."

WAR OF WORDS

Sloann naturally did not take kindly to the GU's announcement and its accusation of psychological manipulation. Within days, he retaliated by suing GU and its board for defamation of character. Further, he was granted interviews with print, electronic and multi-band microwave visi-channels. In each of which he ridiculed both Son-tu and the University for its science-fiction charges of 'subliminal mental telepathy.' To the media's delight, readers, listeners, viewers, voyeurs, and hangers-on of all stripes responded. Some were wildly in favor of and some openly hostile to the ill-defined subject. The individuals almost seemed to be secondary.

Son-tu was deep in thought. *How can I avoid this situation being turned into something that is either irrelevant to the circumstance or merely personal?* She thought back to what had happened on Andivoli. *Oh, yes; a rare electronic medium's neutral host employing a reasonably neutral interview between two distinct perspectives, i.e., personalities. That's it—we can arrange for a debate!*

With the word *neutral* in mind she advised her confederates of a plan to offer a proposition to Sloann. The Chairman gave her a raised-eyebrow look. "What *kind* of proposition?"

"It will be one which will appeal to his ego."

Two days later she entered Sloann's elegant downtown office suite on the top floor of a building which sported his name. Ushered to the inner sanctum, she was instantly greeted with a question obviously designed to put her on the defensive. "Well, my adversarial opponent, are you and your cohorts prepared to make some concessions in order to avoid expensive lawsuits?"

She would lose no time with amenities. "Good to see you, too, Sloann. As I alluded in our brief electronic exchange, I come with neither a white dove nor a sheathed sword, but an offer of engaging in an audio/visual broadcast debate before millions, all conducted by a neutral moderator, the dean of the Department of Philosophy with the oldest and most distinguished secular university on Jun'or. Check him out and give me your answer."

Son-tu knew well that Sloann's single greatest weakness was something he had in common with the many historical figures also wanting the title of King. Her deal-closer before she left the penthouse was this: "This is my invitation for you to join me on a very large stage. You, Sloann the Third, will have the opportunity to present yourself to essentially the entire population of Jun'or."

Sloann trusted no one with much. He did as she suggested, however, and judgment was overridden by ego. The event was set for two weeks hence.

MEANWHILE, BACK AT GAM'MAN UNIVERSITY

The Alphas had come to Bing-ta's office with an incredible story from one of GU's former students who had recently married. The student said he thought the Faith Department heads would be interested in hearing about something in particular, partly because GU's new President was from Andivoli.

Wy took the lead while holding a curious flyer in one of his hands: "Bing-ta, a recently graduated former student of GU said he and his wife received a letter from some real estate organization on Andivoli offering them something the promotional headline obviously borrowed from Earth's Southern Homestead Act of 1865. Here, read it for yourself":

FORTY ACRES AND A MULE – THE OFFER

Well, not 40 acres, and no mule,
but four acres and a two-bedroom/two-bath home,
plus a servant robot on beautiful Lake Andivoli
—FREE—
to any newly married Jun'orian couple
contracting to homestead for five years.

After reading the flyer, Bing-ta exclaimed, "What?! This is on the same lake as my former fishery plant, which I donated to the church. As for the offer itself, it smacks of the imperialist days of Earth's ancient Rome when its citizens were outnumbered by slaves. Roman citizens thrived by virtue of its slave labor. What I see here is a ploy by the Andivolean government to newly-populate the planet with immigrant taxpayers."

Bea was even more worked up than Wy, saying, "Whatever the motivation, it is working. The former student told us they have already signed up, and that some of their friends have as well. If a few newly married couples in just this area have already committed, there must be thousands a-coming."

It was Wy's turn. He shook his head and said to Bing-ta, "That isn't all, my friend. Who do you suppose is partnering with the government on this real estate deal?"

It took only seconds for the light to come on for Bing-ta. "No! You don't mean Sloann!" It wasn't a question, but a statement. He turned up the light, saying, "He wants to be King of *two* planets! Okay, Wy, listen: Son-tu is tied up here on Jun'or with her upcoming public challenge with Sloann. I'm going to take *Boundless* to Andivoli and learn more. My new V.P. can get his feet wet for the next month."

Wy responded without hesitation. "I'll go with you. Bea can cover for me here. Dear," he said in turning to face his wife, "will you bring Son-tu up to speed on all of this?"

"Perfect," Bing-ta said as he flicked a button on his com-glasses before advising his administrative assistant of the plan. He then turned to Wy in asking him to prepare the Andivolean church leaders to assist them upon their arrival.

LET THE PUBLIC DEBATE BEGIN

Son-tu had seen the conflagration with Sloann as an opportunity to take the message of the gospel and the things of eternity to the public in a special way. As expected, Sloann doubled down in taking on Son-tu with her "cultish and anti-world views" and Gam'man University's "divisive and exclusionary" Christian litany. That had led to the moment about which Son-tu was beginning to have reservations with respect to the public's perception of her in such a confrontational witnessing voice. With a bit more reflection, however, she viewed the effort as a staunch stand for Christian apologetics. She would spend the next week in preparation.

Immediately prior to the debate's kick-off, the moderating Dean of the interviewing university made this opening statement: "The Department of Philosophy and Religion at this University is a blended department, offering courses and programs in both of the two separate disciplines. For the viewer's benefit, I emphasize that such pairing of disciplines is reasonable in the sense that both study comprehensive worldviews; that is, differing sets of beliefs purporting to describe the ultimate nature of reality as well as sources of worth, meaning, and purpose in life." That said, the moderator indicated Son-tu would go first in stating her general Christian faith perspective.

Wow! Son-tu thought to herself. *That sounded decidedly pro-secular, but the hand has been dealt.* "Thank you, Master Moderator and ladies and gentlemen throughout the Jun'orian world. Let me begin by stating the Christian definition of mankind: Man was created by the special act of God, in His own image, to have fellowship with Him. But man became alienated in that relationship through sinful disobedience. Only the grace of God can bring a human being into His holy fellowship and enable one to fulfill the creative purpose of God."

"Thank you, Madam Son-tu. Now it is your turn, Master Sloann."

"Let me cut straight to the point with seven words: There is no evidence for God's existence."

The surprised moderator turned to Son-tu and nodded. She quickly saw opportunity and claimed it. "Master Moderator, I know you will allow me to rebut my opponent's baseless claim: Nearly everything the Christian lays eyes on is proof of God's existence, because he or she sees the 'handiwork' of God all around him in creation. There is, however, the ultimate bit of evidence: God made man in His image, and the physical evidence resided in the witnessed presence of Jesus walking on Earth for more than thirty years. The 'chance' of evolution to which my opponent will be referencing, however, has no model.

"Aside from that," she confidently but not stridently continued, "unbelievers simply ignore evidence from anthropology, history, geology, philosophy, and theology. And if by 'evidence' my adversary—let's call an atheist an atheist—means 'that which has come into existence,' he is correct. God never *came* into existence! God always *has been, is, and will be*, simply because He is eternal."

The moderator held up a hand and said, "Master Slo-ann, would you care to respond to that comment, or perhaps introduce a different perspective?"

He did. Again, Sloann chose to be simplistic: "You know, arguments are really nothing but that, and the concept of 'winning' a debate is subjective. But speaking of 'history' it is full of fairy-tales and myths, including the Christian story. And as to yours, *Madam Adversary*, I say, 'logical fallacy'."

"Oh, I see," rebutted Son-tu, not waiting for the moderator's invitation, "You mean such as the *myth* that God the Father sacrificed His own Son in order to destroy death with His life; not to *assuage* His wrath, but to *heal*; not to *protect* mankind from His fury; but to *unite* mankind in His love?"

Son-tu sensed that Sloann was—at that very moment—attempting to focus his outgoing telepathic thoughts to any open minds, even hers. She readied herself for whatever frontal attack might complement that tactic.

"Look to logic," began his new appeal. "Look, if God created the universe, then who created God? To put the point another way, whom did your God consult to enlighten him?"

The moderator: "Madam Son-tu?"

"My opponent forces me to be redundant: God is eternal. If God had a creator, then that God would be God. If God consulted someone, *that* person would be God. God is God for the pure fact that He did *not* have a creator! Our Christian God is the predecessor of all things in creation. Why is God worshipped? Because He is the One who made Heaven, Earth, Jun'or, and Andivoli . . . and created everything else. He is the one and only source *for* everything.

"And I further say to my fellow representative of mankind, that although you call 'logical fallacy' to my argument, it doesn't dismiss the Christian belief system. Those like you who use that argument against Christianity simply fail to grasp what Christians understand as eternal. Look, Sloann, I'm no different than you and all other unbelievers. I, too, am a sinner. In the eyes of God, we're all sinners. But Jesus willingly took our place. God loves you so much that He's already paid the price. He just wants you to experience the gift of forgiveness. And how do you do that? You do it by believing."

It was at that moment that Sloann, who had been failing in terms of his mental telepathic power, mistook the apparent compassion of his opponent as a weakness. In fact, Son-tu even felt the force of Sloann's sudden thought resurgence to the point of her blinking not once, but twice,

Perhaps out of desperation, he closed the debate/interview ominously and with a threat. "You may feel you have gotten the better of me with your clichéd arguments, but I tell you that any grace you think you may have gained will indeed be costly." There was then a pause before the adversary fired off his closing line with a shout, conveyed with nothing less than sheer malevolence: "Until then, cursed Son-tu of Andivoli, damn your God and His so-called Spirit!"

That evening, as Son-tu and Bing-ta sat for dinner, she said, "I feel sorry for that man, because in his having rejected the prompting of the Holy Spirit he has removed himself from the only force that can lead him to repentance and restoration to God."

Bing-ta's comment-in-kind was, "Yes, only those who have turned their backs on God and rejected all faith have any need to worry. And that is simply because they will never ask for forgiveness."

Two days later, news headlines all across Jun'or screamed, *Man Who Publicly Blasphemed God Suffers Heart Attack!* Two weeks later, the follow-up secular story with Sloann had to do with the news of his heart having been artificially replaced and the patient discharged from the hospital without need for further rehabilitation.

FORTY ACRES AND A MULE – THE VISIT

Another two weeks passed before Bing-ta and Wy returned. A meeting was convened for the following morning at Chairman Washington's office. Also present were Son-tu, Bing-ta, and the Alphas. After the favorite local drink had been served, Bing-ta said, "As anticipated, my investigative partner and I would like to make an official report on Andivoli's Great Real Estate Giveaway."

Nearly simultaneously, Son-tu and the Chairman both said, "Go!"

Bing-ta, too, was ready and eager. "Let me spell out the opening gambit," he said, "then Wy will offer additional details. With the help of several of our first-rate Rimerian leaders on Andivoli we visited the lake site— which, as everyone knows, is the very same lake which housed my former fishery. We had already been told by the chief church leader there that the regional ministry had applied Andivoli's almost limitless law of eminent domain in securing the fishery/church property, for which less than fair market value was paid. It had been knocked down and rebuilt as the real estate sales and administration offices for the government's massive 'humanitarian' project. More than two thousand homes have since been built, half of which have already been sold."

Wy was anxious to take his turn. "We visited the real estate offices. Whose name do you suppose is shared on all of the extensive property signage?" With that, he held up a large commercial calendar, from which he read its advertisement:

Welcome to Andivoli-Sloann Estates!
Where Young Lives Get their Free Start . . . and Andivolian Futures Begin

Wy turned to Bing-ta as if handing off a sports ball, using both hands in an imaginary motion. The receiver reciprocated with a smile, a faked catch, and a quip: 'As we all know, there is no such thing as a free lunch.'

"That, however, is what these promoters would have prospects believe. We took a tour of the place by an absurdly feminine-dressed robot. In addition to our quick inspection of one of the demonstration homes, the 'bot showed us blueprints for an elementary school, business cubicles, and a marina. It closed its sales presentation with a document it wanted us to sign, 'merely to express interest by a qualified prospect.'

"Instead, we insisted upon reading the ten-page document on the spot. Included in its trailing lines in four-point type, the disclaimer read, 'When, upon receiving the key to a home and assignment of a personal robot, *any* maintenance fees which might or might not be incurred after the first year can never amount to more than one percent of the purchase price.'" A smirking Wy added, "The potential frequency of the assessment, however, was not disclosed."

"If I may at this point," Son-tu said, "allow me to summarize my reaction. I don't think there is anything we can do to stop this development charade except to hope and pray that Sloann has a living will naming a robot as his nearest of kin." She paused for a beat as devilish smiles spread across everyone's face. She continued: "But one thing we *can* actively do is give all the *hidden facts* of this 'Incredible Nirvana Home Offer' plenty of visibility. In the meantime, folks, do you agree that we have other fish to fry?"

Bing-ta rose to the occasion with a relevant two-word close: "Fish on!"

STAYING THE COURSE

Following her debate, Son-tu had begun a new well-promoted, on-air evangelical series of messages. After the first day's successful introduction she began the second day with this: "Dear listeners and viewers, what can I say to someone who might challenge me with a statement such as the following? 'Not only is there no evidence that Jesus Christ was a real historical figure, but there is also no evidence that God exists!'

"Some of you may know that I recently began a very public discussion on this subject with someone whose name you would readily know. Barely into the debate, however, he bailed. Therefore, I would like to take up where I left off. Not only do we have abundant and incontrovertible evidence which accounts for Jesus being a real man and the son of God from both biblical and non-biblical sources, but there are also numerous accounts of Jesus—in resurrected form—from both Christians and non-believers. The plain fact is that were it not for Christ, Christianity would not exist.

"Now, as to the *evidence* for God, we know that our universe had a beginning. And that fact relies on another fact; that a greater Being than man had to have caused that beginning to take place. As we have just noted, there was literally nothing from which to begin. Now, granted, that if we find no evidence for the Bible stories in archeology, then they are fiction, but the fact is they can't be fiction because the evidence truly *is* there."

She paused a moment to glance at a piece of paper she was holding. "I have here a question sent to me electronically after yesterday's on-air session. Allow me to read it aloud: 'Which event is the more important: Jesus's birth or His death?' That is a great question because the answer is 'yes.' All men and women are born to live, but the life of man is very short; call it temporary. And then comes forever. Folks, Jesus was not only born to die, but both His birth and death are celebrated, unlike for anyone else in history."

She finished the balance of her session and closed by thanking her audience before adding the following: "From now on I will be addressing the most interesting question sent to me following my previous day's message"

The next day's message began with the selected call-in question: "What is the meaning of 'in the fullness of time'? She began her answer: "A gifted musician framed the answer this way:

Love was when God became man,
locked in time and space, without rank or place.
Love was God, born of Jewish kin,
just a carpenter with some fishermen.
Love was when Jesus walked in history,
lovingly He brought a new life that's free.

"So, you see, it was love that prompted God to become a man, to walk in history. However, this was no idle whim or last-minute effort to salvage a corrupted mankind. The

Bible refers to His 'perfect timing' as 'the fullness of time' (Galations 4:4).

"If I may digress a bit, when I came into the studio this morning someone stopped me, saying, 'Over the years I have listened to many of your messages. I am not a Christian but I wonder why it is that you love people like you do?'

"I love that question because the answer is so simple: Because God loves *me*. And He loves you just as much. And because He loves you and me, that is mercy. Mercy rather than the justice we each deserve for having been born dead in sin and trespasses. God recognizes that Christ gives life to those who put their trust in Him. Shouldn't you trust the One who offers you faith through grace?

"If that same person is listening to me now, that offer remains on the table. Thank you for tuning in, folks. Do so again, please. It will also be my privilege to hear from you. May God continue to bless."

And so it went for the next several weeks with So-tu's daily messages and her answers to listener's questions.

WY'S QUESTIONS

One day, Wy asked Bing-ta to meet with him for lunch and conversation. Wy obviously had something on his mind. "Once seated, but before they placed their order, he said, "You know, Bing-ta, I suspect Son-tu and Boxx have shared much with you about Bea and I, but I don't know much about you. Share something unusual about yourself; something that few people would know."

Surprised by his friend taking such interest, he scratched his head and said, "Well, since you put it that way, and because I am fresh back from Earth and the middle-East, let me tell you about one of my American

156

forebears. My grandfather fought in a war not unlike Russia's invasion of Ukraine thirty years ago. Ironically, his service took place thirty years prior to that. He fought with the Third U. S. Army in Iraq in 1990-1991, in what was then referred to as the Gulf War.' His unit was involved in the capture of a Italian-built field cannon, a 2,800 lb., 105 mm howitzer. It was subsequently shipped to the U.S., and ultimately ended up in the state of Georgia with one of my forebears in an American Legion veterans' organizational Post. They affectionately named it 'Howie,' utilizing the cannon in parades and as an advertising and fund-raising tool."

Wy blinked and said, "Now that's what I call a surprising bit of generational background.

Thanks for sharing!"

Bing-ta nodded and said, "Thank you, but the story itself isn't the precise reason I pulled it from my memory banks. In response to your specific question, I am a card-carrying 'Son of the American Legion.' By that, I mean, as a direct descendant of an American military service man, I am an inactive, dues-paying member honoring my grandfather's military service to his country."

Wy had opened the door to something in which he was much more interested, so he walked through it. "All of that is interesting, my friend. I do, however, have something else on my mind. You know that Bea and I go back quite a few years with Son-tu. She and her grandfather became active in the Rimerian Movement shortly after the two of them arrived on Jun'or. You may not know that their trip here was at her urging because she felt called by God to evangelize her grandfather's pagan home planet."

Bing-ta's face sported an amused expression, seemingly expecting something further. He nodded for Wy to continue.

Wy didn't pick up on the nuance and said, "You may not know that Gam'man and my father were best friends long before the misadventure which landed them in a penal colony on one of Jun'or's double moons. It was from there that they managed to escape to Earth via a commandeered orbital maintenance craft. Anyway, you can imagine how protective Bea and I are of Son-tu."

"Ah, so that's why you seemed to have second thoughts about the three of us charging off to Earth together from Andivoli."

"I don't recall that being the primary reason, but to a lesser degree, yes."

With the hint of a smile Bing-ta said, "So, what else is on your mind, Wy?"

"I think you know. The two of you have acquired separate living quarters, but Bea and I are wondering . . ."

Now Bing-ta had to laugh before finishing Wy's sentence for him, "What are my intentions?"

Now it was Wy's turn to laugh. "Bingo!"

"You, sir, are prescient. For some time now I have been rehearsing my marriage proposal. I have broached the subject with her twice before—once on the way back to Andivoli, and once again shortly after we arrived on Jun'or—but in both instances it was simply too soon after Boxx's passing. What is your thought about that at this time?"

Wy couldn't contain his enthusiastic surprise. "Hallelujah, brother! And speaking for both of the Alphas concerning your question, no, it is not too soon to propose! I knew Boxx well enough to know he would have wanted Son-tu to go forward with life."

"Then that is settled between the two of us, which leaves it up to my persuasive abilities with Son-tu. Should she accept, I would like to prevail upon you to be my best man!"

"Done!" With that, however, Wy's tone turned to a more somber note. "Since we have concluded that business, my good man, I would like to know how you are doing. I mean, you would likely be giving up everything on Andivoli. How are you with that?"

"Thank you for asking, but that is demonstrative of your fine empathetic qualities. The fact is this: Aside from a very few good friends, I will miss only one material thing; my sailboat. Here, allow me to show you a photo of it." With that, he pulled the picture from his wallet. "I christened her 'Restful'."

"Wow, what a beautiful craft! I could see myself sailing her."

Bing-ta could tell that Wy was sincere in his admiration of the boat. "I'll tell you what, my good friend; I'll leave it behind for you when I am raptured!" They both fell to laughter.

WILL YOU?

Following Son-tu's next well-received microwave broadcast, she went out to dinner with Bing-ta. Once seated, she said, "Wow! This certainly beats eating on the run!" She was feeling particularly upbeat with the day's earlier broadcast and the excellent questions posed afterward by several viewer-listeners. She placed her com-glasses inside her evening purse and pushed it aside. *How nice. We haven't often done this sort of thing. He is so thoughtful.*

Bing-ta responded by starting a conversation. "I asked Wy about his and Bea's favorite 'break-room' and this was his suggestion." He looked around the room and added, "You know, I think that stage up there is for some kind of local musical talent. In any event, I have taken the liberty of ordering a special hors-d'oeuvre." He looked around again. "Oh, here it comes."

The tuxedoed waiter sat the covered canister down and said with a wink of the eye, "I trust you and your lady will enjoy this, sir."

With a smile on her lips, Son-tu said to her escort, "What makes him think I am *your* lady?"

Bing-ta thought, *what a perfect segue. I know she can't thoughtfully sense my intentions, but I had better get on with it.* "Allow me to answer that, my dear," he replied. Having said that, he reached for the canister and slowly removed the cover to reveal its contents. He then focused on her expression.

Having leaned forward in anticipation of seeing what might be so special, she instantly saw the opened ring box, which led her to clap her hands to her cheeks. With a huge smile, she uttered one word: "No!"

He laughed. "Well, that wasn't what I was looking for, but I have heard it a time or two before. Hey, I love this *lady*! Wilt thou truly be mine, and marry me?"

She jumped up, nearly tipping the table over while shouting, "She will!" They kissed and she whispered, "What has brought this on, Master Bing-ta?"

"To be precise in answering your question, it was Wy."

She pushed him away a tiny bit. "You mean for you to ask me to marry you?"

"No! Silly! He merely said he thought the timing was right and that it wasn't too soon after your having lost dear Boxx. In any event, I will be asking him to be my Best Man."

That provoked her to say," Then Bea will be my Matron of Honor. I am so happy!" She thought for another moment before a serious look crossed her face. "You know, darling, when I did not encourage your first advances during our trip from Earth to Andivoli, you shared

160

some wisdom with me along the lines of 'it's not what happened to a person, it's what is done about it.' Since then, I have given that a lot of thought. It's about time I did something serious about my future. Okay! Now that we have settled that, let's enjoy the evening. I know you want to dance."

"A dance at this very moment will not only be my privilege, but it will be my first since having lost my first wife."

PRECURSOR

It was time for Son-tu's regular broadcast, which would now also be streaming for any interested party's com-glass or personal computer conveyance. "This is Son-tu of Jun'or, by way of Andivoli and Earth, continuing my Christian messaging. First, a program note in that I will be absent from this microphone for a few days. Why? I am getting married! His name is Bing-ta of Andivoli. He is a handsome and wonderful Christian man and former fisherman who some time ago joined my mission—and now after a period of time from having lost my beloved husband, Boxxton—has also joined my personal life.

"The two of us have decided that our wedding will be observed with two key elements in place. One, of course, will be the private ceremony itself. The other will be the accompanying world-wide transmission of the relevant message of marriage between one man and one woman, with Jesus' admonition of his having been forsaken by His eternal Father and that everyone, through faith in Him, need never be forsaken. (Editor's note: A very brief white space now occurs in Son-tu's speech before resuming.)

"I trust you will forgive my momentary digression and succeeding pause, but now I will continue my intended message. The selected audience question from my last session is the following: 'What was John the Baptist's specific role relative to Jesus's coming?' Thank you for that excellent question, caller! It was customary in biblical times for kings to send out a herald, or forerunner. The forerunner's job was to go before his king and announce to the people that the king was coming.

"Let me give you a more modern day example: During a long-ago visit to the President of Earth's United States of America's by visiting leaders of the former Soviet Union and China, it was a given that nations would spend a great deal of money beautifying the highway between the airport and the President's residence. That was something of the case in my biblical instance: "Consider the contrast with the insignificant land of Israel in the obscure village of Bethlehem where a 'Special Child' would be born. That Child was the preexistent Son of God. John the Baptist's responsibility was to announce the new King's coming. John the Baptist's ministry fulfilled the words of the prophet Isaiah, which we read in chapter 40, verses 3-5:

'Listen! It's the voice of someone shouting,
"Clear the way through the wilderness for the LORD!
Make a straight highway through the wasteland for our
God!
Fill in the valleys, and level the mountains and hills,
Straighten the curves, and smooth out the rough places.
Then the glory of the LORD *will be revealed.'*

"Yes, Israel stumbled, but Israel did not stumble such that she should fall. No, for in the very stumbling of Israel, God's redemptive plan for the world and all of humanity would be implemented and all the nations everywhere—on Earth and its colonies—would be blessed. You, too, are greatly blessed, but the key to *accessing* the greatest of those blessings is individual acceptance of the Grantor of such blessings.

"Thank you for being part of today's program. Send me your questions. Until the next time, may God continue to bless you!"

NOT FORSAKEN

The details of the wedding were set. There were no living parents, nor any siblings (nor would Son-tu's three still-inexplicably-estranged adult children be present), but a handful of faculty and the GU board would account for the ceremony's quite limited invited guests. Only the uniting message itself would be viewed by the public.

Wy officiated, taking Son-tu's excerpted and slightly paraphrased message, which she referred to as the 'Rosenthal Recitation'. It had been written long ago by M. J. Rosenthal, one of Earth's premier evangelists of his time and a Jew considered by many as one of the most incredibly anointed Christian writers of his era.

Before the private saying of the couple's vows, Wy carefully and thoughtfully began the message: "Loneliness is tragic, but to be forsaken is far worse. To be forsaken means to be utterly abandoned. Jesus was forsaken to a degree that no other human has ever been known. How is that? He was forsaken utterly and utterly forsaken.

"By whom was He forsaken?" someone asks. "By no fewer than five entities: One: Jesus was forsaken by the very world He had created (John 1:3 and Genesis 1:1). In other words, the world would not *receive* Him (John 1:10).

"Two: Jesus was forsaken by the village in which He lived. In Nazareth, where He spent His childhood and grew into manhood, He could do no miracles because they did not believe in Him (Luke 4:23-24). This sad example illustrates the surprising concept that all too often 'familiarity breeds contempt'.

"Three: Jesus was forsaken by James and his other half-brothers with whom He grew up (Matthew 13:55-56), when it would have been reasonable to have assumed they would embrace Him. However, the Word of God declares they did not believe in Him until after His death, burial, and resurrection (John 7:5).

"Four: Jesus was forsaken by the disciples He trained. Long centuries before the inspired penman wrote in Zechariah 13:7, 'smite the shepherd, and the sheep shall be scattered'. With Jesus' death, the disciples fled in fear and defeat—their world had come unglued.

"Five: Jesus was forsaken by His eternal Father. As Christ hung on the cross between Heaven and Earth, He had to drink the agony of forsakenness. And there on that cruel tree and in the anguish of the moment, the Son of God cried out, 'My God, my God, why hast thou forsaken me?' (Matthew 27:46).

Wy was reaching the close of his lead-in to the vows. "For those in our presence at this moment and for what I believe to be millions virtually observing this aspect, the message wanting to be conveyed by Son-tu and Bing-ta is that Jesus was forsaken so that you and I, through faith in Him, need *never* be forsaken. Here then, is grace; greater than all our sin!"

That was the end of the transmissible portion of the wedding. The actual vows were then seen to as Pastor Wy united the two in holy matrimony. With a wink and a nod following the sacred words he said, "The groom may now kiss the bride." The groom responded; first, with a wink, then by saying, "I know," and finally by sealing the ceremony.

That evening, a moving, recorded call came into the broadcast station: "Madam Son-tu, you are my heroine. I have been listening to your messages for some time, but today, of all days, you spoke directly to my problem. I am a young woman and I just learned that I am pregnant. I cannot imagine I could possibly end the life of the one just beginning his or her life within my body, but I do not know what to do. My boyfriend lost no time in advising me that he has taken himself out of the picture. My parents have written me off for this and other grave mistakes in my life. I feel abandoned; forsaken, as was the Jesus of which you speak. I know you can't help me, but I have no one else to tell."

Even though it was Son-tu's wedding night, the station's night clerk apparently thought it best to advise her of the message. With apologies to Bing-ta, she called the traced number and said in a recording, "Young lady, God has heard of your plight and sent me to help you. You need sympathetic counseling from a Christian crisis pregnancy center. I have made arrangements for you to visit one close to the area in which your call emanated. Whatever charges might result will be billed to me. Go there tomorrow morning and then stay in touch with me."

At that point, someone picked up on the call, saying, "It is me, Madam Son-tu. You have saved my life and that of another."

HONEYMOON

Three days following their wedding, Bing-ta said with a faux-searching expression on his face, "Dear wife, tell me what more is on your mind other than things such as 'Why was I born, why am I living, what do I have and what am I giving?'"

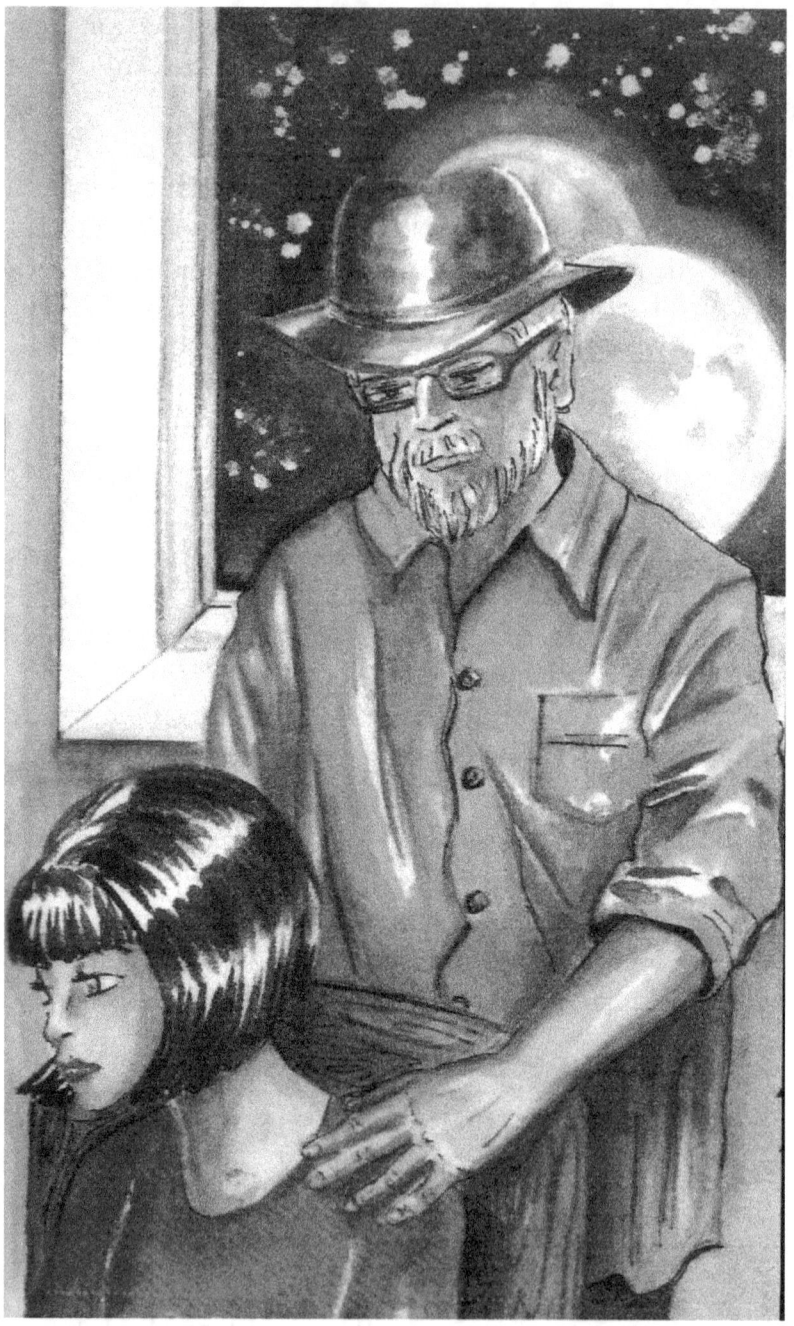

Bing-ta is concerned that something is emotionally bothering Son-tu.

She smiled and nodded, saying, "I could not be happier than that we are a complete couple in Christ. But I will admit that late-night call gave me cause for a deep think. Forgive me, but it was something said before we ever began the mission at which you and I were to meet. It was a sporting cliché which goes like this: 'Players who can, play; those who can't, coach'. I think God has been prodding us to get back to being an active player and not only evangelizers with a message."

He scratched his head, and this time it was with a puzzled expression. "Whatever do you mean by that? We contend for the faith in a positive sense whenever we give our unflinching witness; when we make possible individual discipleship; and with the training of faithful ambassadors for Jesus. You and I are both doing the LORD's work, although on occasion, I have to admit I find myself wondering if my service to Him is more with the lips than with the hands and heart. But don't you think we will finish well and our legacy will be that of strength in our faith in Christ?"

"I understand all of that," she replied, "but how can we finish *really* well? Are we not also meant to go *into* the field rather than merely *sharing* about the field? Was mankind not created to personally glorify God? I mean, dear husband, are we doing our very best to glorify Him? Or is it now our time to actually be out *in* the field?"

Bing-ta blinked twice, frowned, took her into his arms and softly intoned, "Dear Son-tu, humanity can neither add to nor diminish God's glory. In fact, He has proclaimed in Isaiah 42:8, 'My glory will I not give to another'. His glory is accomplished as we allow our lives to be an instrument through which the eternal perfections of God are displayed. I believe we are doing that, but if you feel this is a time for us to go into the field, we can do that. What is your wish?"

Son-tu slumped into his arms, not fainting, but in symbolic praise for her husband's understanding.

He lifted her chin and said, "Do I need a pad and pencil?"

"No! No!" she said as she sat on the bed. "I have only two things in mind. One is to organize a broad humanitarian relief service for Jun'or's hungry and starving people; those who are left bereft of food, either as a result of seemingly never-ending challenges or governments failing to maintain a stable currency, thereby causing the vulnerable to be economically insecure."

Bing-ta cocked his head as if to say 'and number two'?

"That we simultaneously be presenting the message of the gospel. Here's my broader thinking: There are two kinds of overt baptism. The first, of course, is being united with Christ in death to sin and resurrection to new life. As an aside, just as John the Baptist said to the Israelites when he was baptizing in the Jordan River: 'It is not enough to be descended from Abraham; salvation can only be gained by a conscious act of repentance and faith.

Even though we are not Jewish, the second thing is baptism to initiating a new experience."

Bing-ta smiled knowingly. "That is profound, woman. Those were essentially Jesus' final instructions to His disciples."

FIELDS WHITE UNTO THE HARVEST

Within days she had contacted the five largest relief services around the planet, volunteering her/their services in the name of the Rimarian Movement. Four of them immediately accepted, not only for her name, but especially for the skills, experience and contacts well known of both her and the group. The fifth thanked her but did not want what the director bluntly referred to as the group's accompanying "baggage of Christian dogma."

She was able to bring several chief administrators from each of the four organizations to the RM group's modest headquarters to discuss possibilities. Wasting no time in trying to find a common mission consensus, she made a key point: "We have to avoid what one legendary evangelist, Billy Graham, referred to as a 'Trojan horse from the inside', that is, holding strictly to the letter of the law but knowing little of the spirit of love or the Christian graces that belong to a spirit-filled life."

One of the visitors asked her to better explain. She did: "Some well-intentioned groups and churches find themselves busy fighting, bickering, and arguing over small, nonessential points. They have love for the souls of lost people or for the misery of their fellow believers, but they have omitted the social consciousness that was typical of the early church leaders of the 18th century. In other words, they are so busy defending the faith that they have little time for soul-winning. You could even call it Pharisaism.

"On the other hand," she added in offering a qualifier, "there is also Sadduceeism; those who deny the essential doctrines of Christianity. They have a humanistic philosophy that would deny the miraculous character of the Scriptures and have openly rejected the fundamentals of the true Christian faith. Graham summarized it this way: 'The strife and division caused in the Christian church by the Pharisees on the one hand, and the Sadducees on the other hand, have been a stench in the nostrils of God.'"

The relief organization leader who had asked for clarification was now shaking her head in objecting. "I think that if Christ were to come in person today, He would argue against what you are saying."

Son-tu calmly and graciously replied, "Thank you, ma'am, for phrasing your objection in that fashion. In Matthew 23:27, Jesus said, "Woe to you, scribes and Pharisees, hypocrites! For you are like whitewashed tombs which indeed appear beautiful outwardly, but inside are full of dead men's bones and all uncleanness.""

The objector, sincere in her entreaties, asked, "What then are you suggesting we do?"

Son-tu held up three fingers. "First, stand fast in the Scriptures. Second, reexamine the foundations of our faith to be certain we know where we stand. Third, remember that the Word of God predicts just such a time as this."

The upshot of the meeting resulted in unanimous agreement to support one another's resources and communications. They all wanted Son-tu to administratively head what they offered to call the New Rimerian Movement. She was not interested in that, merely wanting to go into the field in doing the work of delivering, sharing, and harvesting . . . alongside her husband.

That, the two did for three years with the able administrative support of the Rimerian Movement's Johnni and Pyoter. Providentially, on the final day of their food and faith field sojourn, a young woman assigned to Son-tu's counseling table said she wanted to share something very personal. After having had an abortion eight years earlier, she and her husband had later been wonderfully blessed with two girls. They were still struggling financially, but the pain, shame and guilt from her abortion had nearly overwhelmed her until she finally found forgiveness and saving grace in Christ.

Son-tu asked, "How did that come about?"

"Thank you for asking. Two years ago, in answer to prayer, I was inspired to find childhood photos of my husband and I. From those I painted a portrait of what I imagined our son would have looked like at about age ten. We named him for the first time and I share my story from time to time at churches in this area. Would you like to see Farley's picture?"

Son-tu was so impressed with the painting and her story that they talked for another hour, sharing with her that most women, including many regularly sitting in church pews, still conceal their past abortions, holding onto shame and guilt. The young woman's parting comment was, "It is difficult to imagine, but I know I will one day see Farley in heaven and ask his forgiveness."

LIFE TAKES YET ANOTHER TURN

Late one afternoon of the evening's long-planned New Rimerian Movement relief services recognition dinner for pastors, teachers and workers, Pyoter breathlessly dashed into Son-tu's and Bing-ta's tent. "The two calmed him down as he said, "Our security team has just averted a catastrophe!"

Before they could say anything, he launched into his report, his hands energized in the telling. "Some guy sitting near the head table before leadership had assembled was acting suspiciously. When two of our men approached him, he bolted. They tackled him, searched him, and found in his possession what at first appeared to be a large, garden-picked potato. It was oddly-shaped, however, and a small metal device was attached at one end. The police hustled the would-be terrorist and his "vegetable" to the police station."

Pyoter had calmed down by now and was able to coherently finish his story. The police exploded what was an obviously well-disguised hand grenade! They said the explosion would have taken out everyone within six meters of the head table. The police are continuing to analyze his brief case and whatever else was in it. The justice system will no doubt see to putting an end to the ironic Jun'orian legal freedoms that allowed a would-be killer opportunity. He will enjoy neither the rest of his life on Jun'or nor through eternity."

Shortly after that harrowing event, Bing-ta sensed in Son-tu a budding malaise. He brought his concern for her out into the open. "My dear, has the last year or so tired you such that your irrepressible enthusiasm in beginning each new day has waned? I seem to detect a faintly suppressed longing for something undefined."

The moment he finished his sentence her expression registered surprise. "What? I am not aware of what you have just suggested. It is true that I have increasingly been having a few wild dreams, but I have never considered dreams to be connected to reality."

He was relieved that there did not seem to be any sort of personal physical challenge, but now he was concerned for what might be emotional. Frowning out of empathy he said, "I bring this up because I sense that something seems to be overtaking you."

His statement startled her. Although she knew him for being the most sincere and unpretentious person she had ever met, she admitted to herself that of late she occasionally found herself screening against undeveloped negative thoughts about life. She shared that thought aloud. "Your word 'overtaken', dear, has somehow been telegraphed to my consciousness."

He blinked in recognizing that this might be the moment for drawing her out. "Talk to me."

"All right, then, let's see if I can sift through it. All I have to go on is a continuing recurrence of my grandfa-

172

ther's and my having crashed into each other's worlds so many years ago. That was when I responded to his telepathic appeal to any maverick UFO occupant who might be harboring deep questions. As you know, I responded telepathically with a five-word question: *'Do you know the Creator?'"*

"You have shared that with me before, but never his answer."

"He was evasive, but encouraging. And that was good enough for me."

"So what do you think is bothering you about that?"

"I don't know for certain, but perhaps that I was missing the previous chapter."

"The 'previous chapter'? What does that mean?"

Son-tu was at a loss to fully explain what had just come to her in answering his question. *Is my problem connected to understanding grandfather's conscious concerns as to whether or not his criminal conviction on Jun'or might impact me?*

"Bing-ta!" she all but shouted. "I think I have just uncovered what has 'overtaken' my subconscious. I need to discover Gam'man's mindset before his escape to Earth."

JUN'OR'S EARLY RISING MOON

A few days later, following some focused research about Jun'or's former moon-site penal colony, Son-tu had learned the following:

> • The moon on which the penal colony at one time housed Gam'man and his two confederates with life sentences for their national currency counterfeiting scheme, is still referred to as "Early Rising," whereas the second of the double moons is known as "Late Rising."

173

• The penal colony was bio-engineered, meaning that since both moons are naturally airless, the penal colony was cocooned in such a physical and chemical fashion as to create artificial gravity and a life-sustaining atmosphere for all it contained.

• Due to political considerations many years later, the penal colony had been shut down, but until just recently remained open to tourism. The tourist appeal had primarily been due to the infamous escape of Gam'man, the senior Chesser, and Sloann-the-first.

• Because the needed energy for the prison was nuclear supplied, however, the facility itself has had to be maintained, otherwise an abandoned reactor's plutonium decay would make the moonscape forever toxic.

Following that, she met with the facility's governmental oversight minister headquartered on Jun'or. Due to Son-tu's generous contributions over the years to Jun'orian interests, as well as her grandfather's founding of Gam'man University, the minister of Jun'or's Early Rising's Governmental Oversight Office begrudgingly acceded to her request to visit the penal facility, but with the stipulation that her husband and a friend would not be allowed to accompany her.

"Master Minister," she began her uninvited appeal, "first of all, thank you for seeing me on such short notice. As you know, I have an urgent need to make this visit to the Penal Colony, but I would be grateful for a further consideration. It is my understanding that my grandfather's and Wy Chesser's grandfather's former incarceration and subsequent escape is part of the reason for the penal colony's having been a profitable government tourist attraction for many years."

With that lead-in, she further advanced her case. "There has come disturbing publicity concerning the family of Phillip Sloann, who was the third escaping member once housed on the colony. Sloann's grandson is the recent Jun'or headliner who publicly blasphemed God. What is the point? I know the voting public would be interested in a follow-up story connecting the three grandsons and their famous grandfathers.

Now it was time for her close. "Your name and photo, sir, will surely come up in the media, whether you make this three-party request possible . . . or deny it."

The minister had heard many persuasive arguments in his lifetime of politics. This one, however, was being dumped into his lap as a positive opportunity with zero downsides. "Based upon your perseverance, Madam Son-tu," he said in walking back his previous decision, "I reverse my course. Will sometime yet this week or the next work for you?"

THE VISIT

The *Boundless* had a new destination some 200,000 kilometers distant. With Son-tu navigating, Bing-ta piloting, and Wy comfortably seated aboard, they lifted off for a short day's hyper-jump to Early Rising.

Shortly after landing just outside the heavily structured and canopied penal institution, the three suited up for entrance to the airless moon's facility. They were met by a similarly suited guide and followed his lead and signage to the air chamber's entrance. Once inside, they were met by someone they presumed to be the facility's maintenance supervisor. He escorted his visitors in single file through the access portal for removal of their transport suits. The visitors could not help but notice that he was surprisingly disinterested in attending to them.

"You see, lady and gentlemen," he began droning some seldom-used but obviously memorized chatter, "there are two maintenan—ah—security officers on duty here for three months at a time. We are referred to as Duty Officers One and Two. I am DO1 and am happy to give you a *short* tour."

Son-tu interrupted him. "Thank you very much, DO1, but if you don't mind, it is the cells occupied by my grandfather Gam'man and Master Chesser's grandfather in which we are interested."

He appeared to be affronted and curtly responded, "In that case, follow me and I will introduce you to DO2." Fifteen minutes later they had descended a full flight and were proceeding down a dank hallway to what appeared to be a staging area of sorts. Another worker was waiting for them. DO1 said, "This gentleman will try to answer any questions you might have. He has been employed here for many years and, in fact, is the grandson of the officer who was in charge of this particular facility's ward at the time of your two grandfathers' incarceration."

Son-tu and Chesser looked at each other as if to say, "This couldn't be better!"

DO2 bowed slightly, "It will be my privilege to be of service. Please follow me." After another twenty-five meters or so they entered a cell and the docent threw a light switch.

"As you know," he said, smiling, "we rarely have visitors these days. A few years ago we had a much larger staff. Even governmental departments are sometimes susceptible to advancing costs amid retreating public interest and values."

Bing-ta was impressed with the docent's welcoming frankness. "Tell me, sir, did your grandfather ever share anything with you concerning any of our three infamous prisoners?"

"Oh, my, yes! Where would you like me to begin?"

This time, all three of the visitors had to work at restraining their enthusiasm, settling for merely blanching at the volunteer's remark. Wy recovered first. "If this was Gam'man's cell, where was Chesser's?"

"Adjacent, of course."

Son-tu's forehead wrinkled as she expressed her curiosity verbally. "Why do you answer my friend's question in that fashion?"

His reply was matter-of-fact: "How else could they have managed to dig a tunnel between them?"

With that unexpected response, Son-tu asked if the four of them might sit for further conversation. Their helpful guide dutifully took a few minutes to locate and set up a small table and four crudely carved wooden stools in the better-lit hallway outside the cell.

He then resumed his penal colony litany about which he said he knew better than anyone alive. "Ma'am," he began, "if you don't mind, would you share with me what you believe are the facts concerning the fabled escape of the three; the *only* prisoners to have ever escaped the blue-collared Early Rising Penal Colony's Prison and Re-hab Facility."

"Well," she hesitated a moment, "I don't know much, because my grandfather clearly did not like to talk about the experience. This is what I recall: After about two years into their lifetime sentences, my father said he used their twice-weekly library privilege to devise an escape plan for the three of them. It involved a clever scheme to overcome the loosely organized cleaning team and donning their uniforms and face masks. From there, he said they made their way to the decommissioned inter-planetary space craft which had just been converted to a moon-orbit maintenance role. Oddly enough, the library apparently had some astronomical charts to abet their multi-year flight aboard what must have been a well-provisioned space craft. There, that's what I know!"

The docent nodded passively and asked a question. "Do you know anything about our library?"

"No. Why?"

"Frankly, it was quite a facility, and given our clear-sky atmosphere, it also housed at that time a top-level observatory and a world-class electronic library. Scientists routinely came here for astronomical study purposes. Detailed planetary maps were part of its extensive collection of *The Annals of the Universe*. In addition to your grandfather, the other two of our infamous prisoners were also regular visitors."

Son-tu looked at the other three, nodded, and said, "All three were engineers."

"Yes" the docent confirmed, "and all three were quick studies. But the broader escape plan was much less complicated than the transfer and destination aspects. What do you know about those elements?"

Son-tu probed her memory. "I only remember the telling as a few bullet points:

- There was lax security on account of its paper-crime population being isolated on an airless body.

- Again, the three somehow overpowered a cleaning team, switched uniforms, smoothly exited the facility, and boarded the space craft.

- And, as my grandfather liked to phrase it, 'With a push of a button, they powered up and out of the hangar and onward towards destination Earth'."

Wy frowned at the brevity described by her final point. "Wait a minute," he said, "don't tell me you buy the story my grandfather passed down about their interstellar transit having taken seven years with only a bag of carrot chips to eat!"

It was Son-tu's turn to frown. "I don't know, but what I was told about that was this: Once they escaped the moon's weak gravitational field, the former inter-planetary spacecraft took seven years in the automatically piloted ship as the three lay motionless in stasis. Apparently the craft possessed an experimental system allowing for automatic flow of blood, fluids, and oxygen, as well as programmed muscle toning until such time of precise revitalization for orbital arrival."

She quickly qualified what she had just said. "Now, I personally think much of that is a lot of hooey, but the fact is that all three made it to Earth. End of that part of the story."

DO2 laughed. "I love the creativity. And some of it is correct; at least the part about the access to the library, the cleaning team escape, and even the commandeering of the space craft, but not the seven-year, stellar flight-and-stasis fable."

Son-tu and Chesser looked at each other like two cows staring at a new gate. "What?!" they said, incredulously and nearly simultaneously.

The docent shook his head before continuing to correct their tale. "Look, Jun'or doesn't possess such a stacis-travel concept today, much less back then, but there is more to tell. The orbital maintenance craft was fairly new and well-outfitted, but they first made it to Andivoli. Andivoli had only recently been colonized and was friendly with its sister planet, Jun'or. There was no reason not to help Earth-bound travelers in need of help, so they outfitted the three for the planetary hyper jump of about ten days."

The docent was thoroughly enjoying the conversation. "Understand that when the three departed for Earth, they were fugitives. As we much later learned, they somehow managed to set down in Earth's Arizona desert, secrete their ship, and meld into a hermit beginning before much later striking out on their separate paths."

Son-tu shook her head in disbelief as she looked to Chesser for verbal support. His reaction, however, was totally opposite hers.

"Wait a minute, Son-tu, I think this makes a whole lot more sense than the science-fiction fodder they fed us."

"Bing-ta?" she said, her eyebrows still raised as she queried her husband.

Bing-ta shrugged. "I'm with the Jun'or docent's grandfather and grandson Chesser. That's three-to-one, my dear."

Always quick to recover from a set-back, she smiled in capitulation and said, "Look, I'll go with 'whatever'. Let's see what else we can learn from the proxy holder."

DO2 gave up a smirk along with a little sarcasm. "I'm standing right here, you know. What else can I do for you?"

Wy had wandered a few meters away from the hallway and into one of the two cells. He was searching the walls with eyes and fingers and said, "I'm wondering if any of the three ever etched anything onto the rock walls."

The docent nodded. "I don't know anything specific about that, but I do know that all prisoners attempt to mark the passage of time. A man locked up can't help but do that. The facility's policy, however, had always been to either remove or paint over cell wall marks whenever a cell was vacated."

Son-tu shifted her thinking. *What had the docent said earlier about Gam'man and Chesser having tunneled between their two cells?* "DO2, how did the tunnel figure into the escape?"

That question apparently hit a nerve because it caused the facility's knowledgeable and helpful docent to suddenly put one hand to his mouth.

"What is it, sir?" Son-tu asked. "Are you okay?"

"I am, thank you, but you have hit on a crucial and little known element. Not only was there no connection between that tunnel and their escape, but the tunnel was never discovered!"

"Never discovered!"exclaimed a confused Chesser.

The docent looked around and said, "Strange. Anyone else hear that echo?"

Bing-ta covered for Chesser, saying, "Sorry, sir, he doesn't get out much."

Everyone laughed and the docent continued. "That is the mystery, and I'll explain it. They did *complete* a tunnel, which allowed your grandfathers to encourage one another." At that, he paused and wiped an eye. "I have never shared this with anyone else, but I will tell you folks. My grandfather told me he knew of the tunnel, but that he did not report it. Why not? Quite simply, because he knew that a tunnel only between the two men could not lead to an escape, yet it would help keep each other's spirit alive."

At that statement, Son-tu's eyes required her to pull a tissue from her side-pack.

The docent, however, wasn't through with his forthcoming and heretofore secret commentary. "But that isn't what still speaks so loudly to me."

The three visitors, moved by his previous revelation, waited in anticipation of whatever conclusion might be coming.

"Your two forebears had an obviously good plan for escape, but they also knew that if the tunnel were discovered after their exit, the authorities would blame *my* grandfather; perhaps even execute him. Knowing that as a possibility, immediately following the escape, he anxiously ran to the cells where he discovered that the two had destroyed the tunnel. How did they manage that? Each apparently began what must have been an arduous effort at refilling the tunnel from each of their half-way points. They thus would have had to work backwards, perhaps for six months or better in concealing their original work. For that gracious effort, lady and gentlemen, I am as grateful to them as was my grandfather." The visitors quickly stepped forward to congratulate him and Son-tu even offered up a hug.

It was time to leave, but Bing-ta, having less of an investment in emotion than the other two, posed one final question. "DO2, I know it is common for prisoners to contemplate escape, but from where did these two men find early motivation, given the reasonable possibility that they might otherwise . . . someday . . . likely gain pardons?"

At that question the docent smiled broadly. "Are you folks going to pry *everything* loose from this tired, old maintenance worker? Look, I've mentioned that at that time the prison housed a first class library. In fact, the warden had compiled and listed 150 titles in our library at the time, of his opinion as to the greatest books ever written. Granted, he was a reader, but he was also in charge of doling out a book here and there.

"When your two ancestors had been here for nearly a year—as my grandfather shared with me—he saw in them the potential for redemption. He took them two books. The first was a copy of the *Holy Bible*, in which he wrote each of their two names, along with these words: 'Here is hope for the *next* life.'"

That brought an audible gasp from the visitors.

"But wait," he said, "you could likely never guess the title of the second book. Care to try?"

The three looked at one another in a fashion that was becoming common among them during this trip. Finally, Wy ventured a guess: "Homer's *The Iliad*?"

Bing-ta jumped into the guessing game: "I'll go with Hemingway's *The Old Man and the Sea.*"

"Madam Son-tu," their guide said, "would you care to hazard a guess?"

"Thank you, kind sir. Let me see; so many from which to surmise. I'll go with *Doctor Zhivago* by Boris Pasternak."

"Good guesses, all of them, but off the mark! It was *The Count of Monte Cristo* by Alexandre Dumas. My father again wrote the two prisoners' names in it, but with *these* additional words: 'Here may be hope in *this* life.'"

"Why that particular book?" questioned Prof. Chesser, the best-read member of the group.

"Gotcha!" said the gleeful docent. "The clue is in *wh*at he wrote: 'There's hope in *this* life!' You have probably all read some of Dumas' work, but this one is the thrilling adventure tale of Edmond Dantès, claimed to be one of the most widely read romantic novels of all time. It is set against the turbulent years of the Napoleonic era. Now, if you have read it, you may recall the protagonist's great challenge: He had been betrayed by his enemies and thrown into a secret dungeon, doomed to spend the rest of his life in a dank prison cell.

"Bear with me," the orator of the mystery said as he continued to play the line and its bait. "Fourteen long years of intolerable captivity finally ends in a miraculous escape in a most ingenious fashion. That story did actually involve a tunnel escape, but also the placement of Dantés in the body bag of the careless guard he killed and threw into the sea.

"And here is the closer: It was my grandfather's notion that that book's incredible escape episode is not only what rendered Dumas' story immortal, but was the inspiration for the creative thinking and daring execution that saved your ancestor's lives."

BACK FROM THE MOON

Back at the University compound a few days later, Bing-ta and Son-tu shared with Wy and Bea their decision to send a modest sum to DO2 in appreciation for his very special sharing and his grandfather's long-ago support for the imprisoned adventurers.

During that surprising and enlightening moon-side interlude, Bea said she had several times attempted to telepathically reach Son-tu, but for some reason had failed. Son-tu nodded sympathetically, saying "That has happened to me on occasion. The usual explanation is that the intended recipient is too focused on something for external mental thoughts to enter his or her mind." To that she added, "Sorry, Bea, but I'm here now and I'm all ears as to what you were about."

Bea could hardly conceal her excitement. "It wasn't an emergency, but I knew you would want to know right away. Three has just applied to GU!"

Son-tu all but fainted! All she could immediately say after steadying herself was, "What?" Turning to Bing-ta, she said, "After all these years of estrangement with Boxx's and my oldest son and his wife and their home schooling of Three in a rural area three time zones away, and I suddenly have a grandson a-calling, I hardly know what else to say except . . . wait a minute . . . I recall that his father's reply card to our wedding invitation did say something about wanting to to visit when we returned to Jun'or.' Frankly, I had heard that before and so I didn't take it seriously."

Bing-ta laughed and brightened at the exceptional news. Apparently wanting to know more about his sudden and hopeful 'grandfatherly' role, he asked the obvious question, "What's with the 'Three' moniker?"

Son-tu grimaced and said, "I'm sorry. I should have been more forthcoming. First, there was grandfather Gam'man; then the abducted and long-departed, bastard son, Gam'man, Jr.—my biological, if clinical, father—and then me. I was followed by my son, Ronnal—named after Boxx's father and J. Ronnal Tolkien, and now Ronnal's son; Gam'man the third, called 'Three.'" "Sadly, I have only been allowed to see him on occasional birthdays."

Tight-lipped and eye-moistened, Son-tu chose to shed a little more light on family. "A sorry argument once took place between my son's wife and I over her insistence on Three's natural delivery at home versus her refusal to at least employ a mid-wife. The boy subsequently suffered several health challenges in the delivery and was in neonatal recovery for months. Ironically, I was blamed for not having seen to there being a physician at hand during birth."

With that explanation having been made, she turned to Bea and said, "May I see his application?" Bea had it at hand and proudly produced it. Son-tu quickly devoured its contents while her thoughts rambled: *He won't turn seventeen until the fall and he wants to be admitted then. Let's see what else is going on. H'mm, no problem with grades! His elective essay on Louis Pasteur suggests he is the precocious lad for which I had him pegged at an early age. Well, his written response to 'What are some of your goals in life?' are interesting.*

She decided to immediately make an effort to contact the family. Using a private com-glass wavelength, she made an inquiry to her son. Expecting little response, she was shocked at both her son's greeting and reaction. As if they had been regularly communicating with one another for some time, he simply said, "At Three's repeated insistence we have been following your broadcast messages. After the most recent one he said that after graduation he wants to enroll at GU and pursue a major in Uncle Wy's and Aunt Bea's Christian Faith Department."

Son-tu was momentarily tongue-tied, not only at the statement, but even more so with her son's familial response. She quickly cut to the heart of the family's long-time source of estrangement: "Ronnie, is your wife aboard on this?

"Yes, and I'm glad you asked. "I am truly sorry for much in the past between us, but things have dramatically changed on this end." Then came the blockbuster: "All three of us have recently come to a Christian faith belief, but it is Three who wants to also pursue his faith intellectually."

Son-tu could barely contain her excitement. "Look, son, I have seen many turns in people's lives, but none more important to me than what you have just shared. Get yourselves back here as soon as possible for a visit, and let us begin again! I want you to meet Bing-ta and I want to love on the two of you and Three."

A month later, the blended family of five had assembled prior to Three's freshman orientation at GU. "So, grandmama," the grandson said, "I have a leading question." With that, he lined a hard serve into Son-tu's emotional forecourt: "Now that I am a budding adult, how does one judge what he thinks is a calling?"

Her first thought was, *It is apparent that my grandson, too, has inherited the Jun'orian curse of mental telepathy. Both he and my son, however, continue to block even my minimalist probes.* "A calling? What kind of calling?" she said in returning conversational service with a high lob, along with a slight raising of her head and voice.

Son-tu's son and daughter-in-law traded glances with each other as if to say, "Here it comes!"

The grandson, however, returned the lob with a similar stroke. His response being a question no more profound or probing than this: "Grandmama, what do you know of Louis Pasteur?"

Son-tu put a thumb and forefinger to her chin, having expected something to have come racing in just over the net. "Is this relevant to our subject or are you merely fishing?"

The boy laughed and said, "You will see."

"Okay. I will play your game. As you no doubt know, else you would not be asking the question, young faux barrister, Pasteur was an Earth-French chemist and microbiologist renowned for his discoveries of the principles of fermentation and pasteurization in understanding the prevention of diseases."

"Yes, ma'am, I do know that, but what I do not fully understand is an idiom history quotes him as having said more than 200 years ago: 'Chance favors the prepared mind.'"

He gets an 'A' for an excellent question. Now let us pursue the answer. "Well asked, grandson. Okay. Consider that if a person properly sets himself up for success in a particular area of life, which do you suppose is more likely to aid him in that effort—luck or preparation? Of course you already know the answer; that the chance of having success *does* favor the prepared mind. Indeed, history is filled with stories of great discoveries that involved a seeming gift for finding good things accidentally, i.e., serendipitously; but that is anomalous."

"Yes, I see that, too," he replied. "In other words, the more prepared or knowledgeable one is, the more likely he or she is able to make the most of chance opportunities and observations."

"Well summarized. Now what is your point?"

"Well, aside from how profound are those five little words you just uttered, I see the need to be underway with preparation for a life such as you, grandmama Son-tu, and new step-grandpapa Bing-ta, and Aunt Bea and Uncle Wy, are all leading."

At that, her thoughts again went rambling: *My, how history sometimes reaches out from the past to influence the future. Thank you, Dr. Pasteur!* "So, grandson, you feel you are actually being called to a life of service to your LORD and Savior? You are not too young to make that statement, and I am proud of it, but *admiring* either a fine horse or a sleek sports car are not the same as *owning* one. I suggest we begin with a public affirmation of your faith followed by something symbolic."

The young man said, "Bingo! Baptism!"

Son-tu smiled. "I believe that using *Bingo!* as an inter-rogative will be appreciated by your newgrandpapa! We will see to your wish for undergoing believer's baptism."

ONCE AGAIN, INTO THE FRAY

After a priceless visit with Three and his parents, Son-tu and Bing-ta headed to the hinterlands; most areas being rural, some not so much. They both linked up for several months with one particular church's mobile food and faith-sharing ministry. One day, Son-tu was blessed to sit down in counselor mode with a bright-eyed young woman who asked an interesting question: "I am new to reading the Bible and I don't fully understand Jeremiah 29:11 about faith giving us this 'hope of heaven.' To what can I look forward?"

"Thank you for that fine question, my friend. You are very well spoken. Heaven is a different world about which we know very little. It contains God (a spirit), Jesus (a resurrected body), and the believers who have gone on before. It will contain the spirits of you and all other believers who will eventually pass. "But here's the thing," Counselor Son-tu added, "It is true that we are meant to use our intellect to study God's Word—just as you are doing—but only God can grant us revelation. Jesus' human body was nailed to the cross by the hands of Godless men who put Him to death. But since it was impossible for Him to be held in death's power, God raised Him up again. It is your faith and mine that has put an end to the agony of death, and it is that which will grant us entry to heaven. Now, what greater hope than that could one have?"

The young woman stated she certainly wanted the hope described and was willing to accept Christ's offer. After Son-tu prayed them out a few minutes later, the new believer said, "I leave here with the hope I did not have when I came in. Thank you for that spiritual support much more than for this box of food, which I also need."

It was on that same visit that Bing-ta, too, found himself counseling. His assignment was with an unbeliever who stated that he had come only for the food, but that he did not believe in "the Christian religion." Bing-ta began gently sharing the difference between a religion and a personal relationship with God. The man asked several good questions before making an admission: "I used to pray to God, but then everyone around me seemed to be bowing down to science. How can a person in this day and age not accept that?"

"That, sir," Bing-ta replied, "is an excellent question. Let me help you: Evolution is a nineteenth-century philosophy that has been destroyed by twentieth-century science. Yet the lie continues to be perpetuated, not on scientific grounds, but because it is what morally justifies our immoral society today."

The questioner accorded him only minimal interest, but Bing-ta continued. "A few years ago a teacher of evolution shared something very interesting with me: He stated that he knew the theory of evolution was scientifically impossible, but he was still going to teach it because it was morally comfortable.

"I asked him what he meant by that. He was even more candid, saying that 'evolution' allowed him to live any way he chose. I challenged him on that, explaining that as soon as someone admits there is a Creator, then he becomes morally responsible to that Creator."

Bing-ta's visitor didn't care for that, but admitted he had never thought of life that way.

In an effort to further encourage the visitor, Bing-ta said, "I can sum it up for you with this: Evolution begins and ends with this hopelessly illogical premise: Nothing plus chance equals everything."

The two went on to talk further, but the visitor could not bring himself to make a decision for Christ. As it turned out, the fellow left with a box of food for his table and a discipleship hologram disc for a better understanding of hope for his future.

No one can be argued into heaven, and in fact it commonly takes much more than one introduction to Christ for an individual to receive revelation. Out of that particular experience, Bing-ta was growing in confidence for witnessing to those captured by their unbelief.

Two weeks later, yet another remarkable visit occurred between Son-tu and a woman who, after the counselor had shared with her God's plan for salvation, commented, "Sometimes I think the story of Christianity is right, and at other times I think it's a mix of fables."

Son-tu loved a direct faith challenge and shared something from the Bible about that position: "Elijah once encountered the prophets of Baal, ma'am, and he was arguing with them. At a critical point Elijah stood before the prophets and cried out: 'How long will you rest between two opinions? If you believe the LORD God, follow Him: but if Baal, then follow him.'"

The visitor cocked her head as if to say, "And?"

"I'll read to you what the Bible tells us happened." With that, Son-tu began reading 1 Kings 18:18-35 about the failure of the prophets to awaken their god in accepting Elijah's challenge, ending with the famous verses of 36-38: "Immediately the fire of the LORD flashed down from heaven and burned up the young bull, the wood, the stones, and the dust. It even licked up all the water in the trench!"

The visitor was stunned with the recitation, saying, "That was quite a showdown! I have never before heard that story."

Son-tu closed the conversation by thanking the visitor for being interested and noted, "What better use of one's time than Bible study? You see how Elijah defended his faith. And now you have seen how I defend it before you. How long will *you* rest between the two opinions you brought with you today?"

COLLEGE OF HARD KNOCKS

After Three had completed his first semester at GU, it was the Alphas who came to see Son-tu. She was very much looking forward to getting their report. "I haven't seen much of him lately," she offered and then excused it by adding, "what with our ministry travels. I presume he is doing well."

Wy was not smiling, but Bea spoke first. "Let me give you the same report we shared earlier today with his mother and father: The dear boy managed to pass all of his classes, but barely."

Son-tu was surprised, but then with a bit of thought she shared her gut feeling. "I'm sorry to hear that, but the first time away from home for many first term freshmen is often very different than expected. You know; free time, new friends—or the lack of them—not to mention beer, late nights, living in a dormitory . . . or even worse, some would say . . . a fraternity house. And all of that omits the challenge of making one's own rules. Don't you think he'll snap out of it?"

Wy's expression was still absent a smile, but now he offered a shake of the head. "None of those things are the problem, Son-tu. I know you and Bing-ta have been on the road in far places, evangelizing during the past few months, and Ronnal and his wife are still dealing with new people and jobs themselves, but Three came to us shortly after we saw his grade posting. When we asked him what was going on, he said he thought he might drop out of school."

"Wha-what?" Son-tu stuttered in her reaction. "That can't be! We've seen him with his parents during the recent holidays, and he was very upbeat, saying that things were going great." At that, she paused. "But when I think about that or how he spent his days, he would just blow everything off with 'nothing' statements such as, 'You know, just regular stuff.' He didn't really share anything." She paused for a second before adding, "Hind sight tells me some of the blame is mine. Where was I and my counseling?"

"Well," Bea responded, "don't beat yourself up too badly. We persisted in talking about the situation with him before he literally choked up and said things like, 'No one who isn't part of the Christian Faith Department courses cares a flip about salvation, creationism, cheating, or abortion. And they tell me as much! And not even half of my fellow students in the CF courses actually care either. Everyone thinks I'm either a nerd or a Jesus-freak, or both."

Wy added to Bea's straight forward input: "We, too, tried positive encouragement, but my dear Son-tu, the boy needs some further shoring up before he beaches himself."

Son-tu was beside herself. "My goodness, have I totally misread him, or have I just not been paying close enough attention? Okay, thanks for the heads-up. Give me some time to collect my thoughts. We'll talk again tomorrow."

After several lengthy conversations with her husband that evening, Son-tu and Bing-ta met with the Alphas the first thing in the morning. "Once again, Bea and Wy, thank you," she began. "My noodle has been cooking ever since we talked. In searching for a better recipe for his challenges I believe my grandson has unknowingly given me the key ingredient to solving his problem."

"Oh?" a surprised Bea said. How is that?"

"When he earlier asked me the meaning of Pasteur's phrase, 'chance favors the prepared mind'. I obviously didn't go into it deeply enough. Here is what I think now:

We need to help him and all freshman students by preparing them for dealing with their Christian faith in a world whose secular prince is Satan. I propose starting a new, campus-wide Bible orientation study. I'm thinking a full hour, two nights a week, with foundational gospel and Earth-style pizza. Either first or second semester attendance for freshmen will be mandatory."

The Alphas were immediately all in.

"But," Son-tu added, "there's more: We can split each session equally between gospel essentials and dealing with life's everyday faith nuances."

That word caught Wy's attention. "What do you mean by 'nuances'?"

"Slight variations with life; things that should be specifically addressed at home, but more often than not, aren't. For example, standards of conduct and moral judgment; the *need* for Christian faith; fidelity in relationships and marriage. And if I can get the board to okay it, we might even award a three-hour credit for those with minimal 90% attendance and active class participation.

The Aphas were smiling from one ear to the other as Bea said, "I know who the first sign-up will be, whether he likes it or not."

LIFE ORIENTATION 101

Son-tu opened the course's first class: "Welcome . . . *volunteers* . . . to GU's first Christian Faith Apologetics course." The class laughed at the *volunteer* irony. "We will begin with a simple question: What is the idiom behind this statement, 'Failure to Grow is the Reward for Idleness.' Anyone? . . . anyone? . . . class?"

One young man raised his hand and said," I think that is a trick question, Madam Son-tu. The statement itself is essentially the idiom."

194

"Good response, young man! You are using your listening and analytical skills. The answer is, as you say, quite similar to the question: 'Atrophy is the Reward for Indolence.' What is the point? When it comes to Christian apologetics—that is, when a person's Christian beliefs are challenged—one first needs to understand Christian foundational tenets. Otherwise, you will be swept away. You all know what is referred to as the LORD's Prayer in Matthew 6: 9-15 and Luke 11:1-4, but we should remember that Jesus never prayed it Himself. Rather, it was intended to be instructive.

"Dr. Luke's inspired scriptural writing of the LORD's *model* of prayer is profoundly revealed in the revered 1985 NKJV edition of MacDonald's *Believer's Bible Commentary.* I am deferring to excerpts of that wonderfully insightful commentary for this lesson.

"First of all, the LORD taught the disciples to address God as Our Father. This intimate family relationship was unknown to the believers in the OT. It simply means that believers are now to speak to God as a loving heavenly Father. Next, we are taught to pray that God's name should be hallowed. This expresses the longing of the believer's heart that He should be reverenced, magnified, and adored.

"And in the petition, 'Your kingdom come,' we have a prayer that the day will soon arrive when God will put down the forces of evil and, in the Person of Christ, reign supreme over the earth, where His will shall be done as it is in heaven. We are to live in daily dependence upon Him as the source of every good. Did you get that? We need to rely on Jesus every day, not merely when we have a need or are thanking Him before a meal.

"Then, after we are saved, God deals with us as with children. He will chastise us until we are broken and brought back into fellowship with Him. This forgiveness has to do with fellowship with God, rather than with relationship.

"Now hear this: The plea, 'And do not lead us into temptation' addresses our own proneness to wander and fall into sin. We should pray that the opportunity to sin and the desire to do so should never coincide. The prayer ends with a plea for deliverance—not merely from evil—but from Satan, the evil *one*."

With that examination of the model prayer, which the LORD Jesus gave his disciples, Son-tu took a deep breath before summarizing. "So, then, young men and ladies, that is the introduction to this course, which will be taught by me and Drs. Wy and Bea Chesser, co-heads of the Department of Christian Faith . . . sometimes known informally to the faculty as the Alphas." That statement brought an undercurrent of positive murmurings.

"Much of what I want to share with you for the balance of this lesson was taught to me by someone I regard as one of my Christian reading mentors, Dr. M. J. Rosenthal of Earth. So, with your com-glass recorder set, here we go:

"Every crushed heart, every broken body, every disturbed mind—the collective tears of the human race can trace their roots back to the sin of Adam and Eve in the Garden of Eden. It is this solitary fact that men and women are set apart from and infinitely higher than the animal creation. It is this same fact which gives to humanity its dignity, nobility, and worth. Animals can think, feel, and do, and like people, they possess intellectual, emotional, and volitional capability, but the animal kingdom cannot extend these capabilities toward the infinite God.

"Here is what accountants refer to as the bottom line and what Christian believers know as truth: Because human beings were created with the potential for a perfect and eternal relationship with God, the worth and dignity of humanity can only be understood to the degree that the greatness of God is comprehended."

She stopped her monologue for several beats before her closing lines on the subject and the plan for going forward. "Grace by faith alone in the LORD Jesus is God's gift to humanity. Through that gift we are freed from the consequences of our sins and its penalty – eternal damnation – and given new life, eternal life, in God the Son.

"Now, young men and women, we will end this first class with a brief, poetic summary of the first chapter of Genesis. It tells us that God is not just the Coordinator of natural forces, but that He is the LORD of Creation, the Almighty God. And because He is all-powerful, we should stand in awe of Him and revere Him in all we do.

"Lastly, I know you will have many questions following each teaching session, and we will be available to address them, but this is a series designed to cover a great deal of material. Once again, our goal through this course is to teach you the foundational elements of Christianity and an understanding as to why your faith is named after our LORD and Savior, Jesus the Christ. Manmade religion, on the other hand, can never satisfy or quench the deepest needs of the soul.

"I want to take these last few minutes of our first session to offer each of you special encouragement. There are numerous Biblical verses containing the words 'thus far'. The incomparable Charles Spurgeon points out that those words are like a hand pointing in the direction of the past. In other words, 'thus far has the LORD helped.'

"In more closely examining those last six words, consider how someone coming to a certain point who writes the words 'thus far' has not yet come to the end of the road, for he or she still has some distance to travel. There are still more trials, joys, temptations, battles, defeats, victories, prayers, answers, toils, and strengths to come."

As she was speaking, she looked directly at Three, whose smile was nearly stretching from one ear to the other.

"Inevitably, however, these life experiences are then followed by sickness, old age, disease, and death. But take heart, young folks, for there are other things yet to come. For example, there is arising in the likeness of Jesus thrones, harps, and the singing of psalms, being clothed in white garments, seeing the face of Jesus, sharing fellowship with fellow believers, and also experiencing the glory of God, the fullness of the things of eternity, and infinite joy."

She paused. "I know this is a lot to take in, but it is a big part of what you will or will not become with time. And finally on this subject, how does Psalm 27:4 express these things? With thanksgiving and confidence, lift your voice in praise . . . for the LORD who thus far has helped you, will help you through all your journey."

The first term's course classes would proceed in dealing with the essentials of the Christian faith, including the Old Testament's foreshadowing the New Testament as well as foundational subjects such as salvation, creationism, baptism, communion, the sanctity of life and marriage, and the expectation of unborn babies' right to life.

After class the final day of the course's first teaching, Three came up to Son-tu and said, "Grandmama, I have been wanting to tell you about the most important moment for me in recognizing my decision to stay the course.

"It came early in the course when one boy admitted in class that his friends told him a young person would be foolish to take the gamble Christianity required. I uneasily looked around the room because he was literally speaking for me. But your answer spoke *to* me. You quoted Jim Elliot, the famous young American Christian missionary killed during his attempt to evangelize an indigenous people's tribe of a South American country called Ecuador: 'He is no fool who gives what he cannot keep, to gain what he cannot lose.' You said that he, his Christian mission, and his words have since been memorialized around that world and this one."

To that, nothing else needed to be said. She smiled, gave her grandson a hug, and released him to life.

EPILOGUE

I recall my long-time Bible mentor's surprising comment after having read the third book of my trilogy in 2011, saying, "And you have left it open for the next book." I had given that idea no thought before or since, until the middle of April of 2022. I woke up one morning, blinked, and Minister-in-the-Marketplace, Wayne Clark's words were suddenly in my head.

Along with them were words of the story's heroine, Son-tu, who would be given these words to say: "In time, people will grab hold of the sleeve of a Rimerian Movement member, hold tight, and say, 'What you have, we want, for we have heard that God is with you.'"

This story is one of the results of the gift of evangelism, given to this author by the Holy Spirit. All I have had to do in valuing the gift is to develop and employ it.

In time, all the characters of this story would either find their way to Heaven's narrow gate and eternity in the presence of God, or to wander endlessly without the former. Concerning the latter (the spiritually dead), they are insensible to the things of God and ignorant of spiritual realities (1 Cor. 2:14). A spiritually dead person does not know God and cannot please God (Rom. 8:8). In fact, they want to please themselves, not God (Phil. 2:24).

On the other hand, at the moment a person gives his or her self over to God—the very moment of conversion—the Holy Spirit regenerates, baptizes (fills/identifies), indwells, and seals that person.

May God forever be praised and His children do Him honor for His glory.

-END-

About the Author

Father and son Terry and his two younger brothers on their way to church after the mother snapped this shot in Iowa in1948.

After a two-year stint in the U.S. Army's Signal Corps, Terry was educated in the physical sciences. He forsook that teaching, however, for a career in advertising, following in the footsteps of his father and grandfather. His interest in writing also quickly came to the fore, and he was given an invitation to begin what would become a five-year long monthly column in his industry's premier magazine.

Although he was introduced to church and Sunday school at an early age, he never acquired a personal relationship with the Almighty until God revealed Himself to Terry at age 58. At the time, the then-skeptic was mired in a sense of knowing that something was terribly missing in an otherwise wonderful combination of marriage, family, health, job, and a decent golf handicap.

Led to write his second book, a golf novel about one man's faith matched against doubt, ignorance and pride, he found himself out of his depth. In the process of turning to the Holy Bible in serious research, he came to accept Christ as his LORD and Savior. Over the past twenty-five years he has published more than 150 issues of a bi-monthly evangelical Christian newsletter and sixteen Christian books, half of them inspirational narratives and the other half novels.

The 'gentle naturalist' and opportunist Charles Darwin created—in an almost untrodden field of inquiry—a grand deep time evolutionary theory on the origin of species. Dodd, however, relies on the singular Witness and Word of the Author of Life, who inspired Moses's writing of Genesis 1:1-11. From that, Dodd points out, we can be certain of our dignity and worth because we have been created in the image of God.

Aside from the above, his special interests have included serving as President of GAPPP (Georgia Association of Promotional Product Professionals), two Walk to Emmaus teams, leadership in a long-time men's Bible study, occasionally teaching adult education classes at his church, and he currently serves as Public Affairs Officer with American Legion Post 307. His recreational interests these days are pitching horseshoes, throwing darts, and playing bridge. "All of that," Dodd says, "along with two blessed marriages, a loving blended family, and the inspiration which God has given me to write about the Kingdom, has provided me with an embarrassment of riches."

Mr. Dodd is a writer in Georgia.
His website is terrygdoddbooks.com and he can be
reached at dodd@bellsouth.net

Sources Cited

- Bible quotations taken from various Bible translations, including the NKJV, NLT, NIV
- Rosenthal, Marvin, *Zion's Fire* Magazine, *Divine Design: God's Master Plan for Planet Earth:* Zion's Hope, Winter Garden, FL, Nov-Dec 2021
- John D. Morris, *The Young Earth, The Real History of the Earth: Past, Present, Future*: Master Books, Green Forest, AR, June 1994
- Nathaniel T. Jeanson, *Traced, Human DNA's Big Surprise:* Master Books, Green Forest, AR, March 2022.
- R.B. Kuter, *The President's Bible, When I Am President*, URLink Print & Media, Cheyenne, WY, 2019

- Rod Zwemke, *How Else Will They Know, Attributes of God*, pp 147-149, 2021
- Thaxton/Bradley/Olsen/Tour/Meyer/Wells/Gonzalez/Miller, *The Mystery of Life's Origin: The Continuing Controversy: I1. Summary and Conclusion*, Discovery Institute, Seattle, WA, 2020
- Nathaniel T. Jeanson, *Replacing Darwin, The New Origin of Species*, Master Books, Green Forest, AR, 2017
- Dietrich Bonhoeffer, *The Cost of* Discipleship, Touchstone, NY, 1959
- Thomas L. Robinson, *Jesus and His Times*, The Reader's Digest Association, Pleasantville, NY/Montreal, 1987

- Dietrich Bonhoeffer, *Ethics*, Touchstone, NY, 1955
- Ray Comfort, *Intelligent Design vs. Evolution*, Bridge-Logos, Orlando, FL, 2006

- Terry Dodd, *Mirror Magic, Warning: Advertising Can Be Hazardous To Free Will*, Yawn's Publishing, Canton, GA, 2015
- Isaac Asimov, *Foundation and Earth*, Del Rey, NY, 2020
- Wayne Clark, *Eschaton, A Study of the End Times*, Pleasant Word, Enumclaw, WA, 2008

- Ron Carlson/Ed Decker, *Fast Facts on False Teachings*, Harvest House Publishers, Eugene, OR, 1994
- John Chau, *The Voice of the Martyrs, Who will take my place? VOA*, Bartlesville, OK, June2022
- Alan W. Dowd, *The American Legion Magazine, A Senseless War (Ukraine)*, The American Legion, May 2022
- Joanna Stern, *The Future of Everything, Seeing a New (Augmented) Reality*, THE WALL STREET JOURNAL, May 12, 2022
- Lorraine Murray, *Living & Faith Values, Rejecting Satan's Empty Promises No Joking Matter*, Atlanta C & J, April 2022

- Billy Graham, *When the Spirit of God Fell on an Entire People*, Decision Magazine, March 2022
- Kenneth H. Cooper, *Body and Soul, How to Live a Long Life to the Fullest*, Decision Magazine, March 2022
- Danny Faulkner, *Answers in Genesis Magazine, The Moon*, AIG, 2022
- Serhy Yekelchyk, *Historical Memory Starkly Divides Ukraine from Russia*, THE WALL STREET JOURNAL, April 9-10, 2022
- Lee Strobel, *The Case for Life After Death*, Decision Magazine, BGEA, April 2022

- Steve Herzig, *The Giant: A Preview of Revelation 13?*, Israel My Glory, March-April 2022
- David M. Levy, *The Continuing Conflict, Israel My Glory* Magazine, July/August 2022
- Harry A. Ironside, *At Long Last, Born Again,* Decision Magazine, February 2022
- Garrison Keillor, *Prairie Home Companion Quip List, 2022*
- Billy Graham, *Prepare for the Storm*, Decision Magazine, May 2022

- Louis Pasteur, *Chance Favors the Prepared Mind,* Wikipedia
- Murray Tilles, *The Cup of Elijah,* Light of Messiah Ministries, April 2022
- Christian Defenders; Equipping Christians to Defend the Faith, *Five Objections Atheists Have Against Christianity, 2022*
- L. B. Cowman, *Streams in the Desert,* Zondervan, Grand Rapids, MI, 1997
- National Center for Science Education, *Young Earth Creationism*, NCSE Newsletter, January 22, 2016

- Michael Brendon Dougherty, *The Modest Burden of Life.* National Review, June 27, 2022
- Dylan Pahman & Alexander William Salter, *In God—and Sound Money—We Trust,* Houses of Worship, WALL STREET JOUNAL, June, 2022
- Tmara D. Fickas, *Jim Elliot Biography,* Trending Post, April 24, 2012
- Savior Machine, *The World in His Hands,* Picture/Quote, ("Free Photos"), May 9, 2008
- *War In Heaven,* Shutterstock (from "Free Photos" selection)

- Will Graham. *The Tasmania Devils*, ("Comparison to Barabbas"), Decision Magazine, July-August 2022
- David M. Levy, *The Continuing Conflict*, Decision Magazine, July/August 2022
- Marvin J .Rosenthal, *The Wonder of the Word*, Zion's Fire Magazine, March-April 2022

Other Books by Terry Dodd

(Most of these titles are available online in print format from Amazon, Barnes & Noble, and Canton, Georgia publisher, Yawn's Publishing)

BRIDGE: An inspirational Christian narrative about the things of eternity.

ANCESTORS: A historical novel of a window into the lives of Adam and Eve and other ancestors.

THE CARPENTER: A historical novel about one first century man's struggle with faith.

FIRED WITH ENTHUSIASM: A compilation of true-life stories, treats and humorous illustrations.

THE FOURTH SON: A personal short story about a true life DNA mystery.

THE FOURSOME: A golf novel of one man's faith matched against doubt, ignorance, and pride.

HUNGRY FOR HOPE: A narrative inspired by how we should live, if not by bread.

JOURNEY WITH OUTSTRETCHED HANDS: Foolish things to confound the wise.

LIFE'S TOUGHTEST LESSONS: Such things are meant for something because God is always to be trusted.

THE SEEKER: A romantic business novel about one man's struggle with Christian faith and marriage.

MIRROR MAGIC: A Christian revision of the original title, *Uncommon Influence.*

WHAT A WONDRFUL LIFE: A short, inspirational narrative of and by an 80-year old.

THE GAM'MAN TRILOGY:

UNCOMMON INFLUENCE: A secular novel with a subliminal advertising plot.

ULTIMATE ENCOUNTER: A Christian sci-fi novel questioning whether or not we have ever been alone.

UNTO THE HEAVENS: A sci-fi metaphor for Earth's evils and its rejection of the gospel. (Note: This is the third novel of the Gam'man Trilogy and the lead-in to the series' fourth and final title, *Mission to Mankind.*)

www.ingramcontent.com/pod-product-compliance
Lightning Source LLC
Chambersburg PA
CBHW070700280626
47159CB00022B/1673